NOIR

The Gold Cricket

The Bastard

Cine City

Killer Jazz

JERRY BADER

THE GOLD CRICKET

Detective Joanne Leslie has a fondness for the finer things in life, including the best cocaine money can buy. Unfortunately her lifestyle and a detective's salary don't comfortably coexist. Drug dealer Cheesy Johnston wants his money, cash he needs to replace the five thousand dollars he's paying Jake Klein to get him out of the country. What Cheesy doesn't know is Klein is a bounty hunter tasked with bringing him in for trial.

THE BASTARD

A Russian gangster's wife kidnaps her estranged husband's illegitimate son and murder's the Yakuza affiliated mother in order to protect her own daughter's birthright as sole heir to her husband's substantial legal and illegal business empires. As an adult the bastard son surreptitiously reappears to reclaim his share of his father's fortune.

CINE CITY

A-list actor, Bobby Richards hires a second-rate film producer with a gambling problem to make an art film that's guaranteed to lose money. Richards signs over his rights to the film to his wife in a spiteful attempt to make sure she doesn't get a dime out of their nasty divorce battle, but things don't work out exactly as planned.

KILLER JAZZ

Maurice Delbourne, the jazz musician son of a legendary reggae star and political activist, is targeted for death in LA. Rival Jamaican gangs each backing opposing political parties fear Delbourne might be a populist political option. Can Delbourne's friend and a beautiful waitress stop the gangster's plan, or will Delbourne end up like his father dead on stage in front of his fans.

The Gold Cricket

JERRY BADER

CHEESY

The Final De Linea,
Otay Mesa, San Diego, just north of the USA-Mexican border.

Bail Enforcement Agent, Jake Klein, a handsome aging ex minor league ballplayer, sits at a sleazy bar, nursing a warm beer. At forty-nine, Klein is not all that anxious to be chasing bad guys down back alleys, especially guys like Skinny Cheesy Johnston, but Cheesy, as he is affectionately known in the drug business is about to miss a court appearance, stiffing Klein's boss for a cool half-a-million bond.

Klein's cell phone rings, he answers, "Klein…"
Freddie King: "You ready for the meet."
Jake Klein: "Jesus Freddie, relax, Cheesy will be here when he gets here. Stop calling me."
Freddie King: "You don't bring this prick back, I'm screwed…"
Jake Klein: "I know Freddie. Don't worry. I'll get him."

The front door of the bar opens, a tall lanky drink of water in jeans and a red and black leather motorcycle jacket over a Rob Zombie t-shirt, topped off with a black leather embossed cowboy hat, walks in carrying a brown paper bag. It's Cheesy Johnston. Johnston looks around and spots Klein on the phone at the bar. He approaches Klein.

Jake Klein: "Got to go Honey, my business meeting is about to start."
Freddie King: "He showed up?"
Jake Klein: "Love you to sweetheart." Klein hangs up.
Cheesy Johnston: "You Smith?"
Jake Klein: "I am if you're Skinny?"
Cheesy Johnston: "I don't like it when people call me that."

Jake Klein: "You prefer Cheesy?"
Cheesy Johnston: "Hell no! That's even worse. Call me Clarence that's my real name."
Jake Klein: "Okay, Clarence, you got the money?"

Johnston places the brown paper bag on the bar. Klein opens it and looks. The bag is filled with five thousand dollars as agreed. Klein figures there's no need for Freddie to know about the extra dividend, not that he'd really care, as long as he brought the truant drug dealer in on time to meet his court date. Klein reaches to take the bag but Johnston stops him.

Cheesy Johnston: "You sure this will work?"
Jake Klein: "Oh, it will work all right, as long as we get moving. There's a shift change at four o'clock and my guy will be off duty."

Johnston pushes the bag over to Klein. Klein takes a gold cricket embossed money clip out of his pocket, pulls out a five-dollar bill, and places it under the edge of his unfinished beer. The two men leave the bar. Klein leads Johnston around the back to where he's parked his car. Klein unlocks the trunk.

Jake Klein: "Get in."
Cheesy Johnston: "You gotta be fuck'n kidd'n!"
Jake Klein: "You want to get across the border or not?"
Cheesy Johnston: "Yeah, but I want to make it without suffocating."
Jake Klein: "Don't worry about it. It's only a few minutes to the border and besides I had it ventilated."
Cheesy Johnston: "I don't know about this."
Jake Klein: "Fine... here's your dough..."

Klein shoves the brown paper bag into Cheesy's sunken chest and turns to leave.

Cheesy Johnston: "Jesus Christ! Just hold on…"
Klein turns back, "We going, or not?"

Cheesy hands the brown paper bag back to Klein and awkwardly gets in the trunk. Klein puts his hand on the trunk lid and looks down at Johnston struggling to find a comfortable position.

Jake Klein: "Why don't you have a nice nap and before you know it you'll be in beautiful downtown Tijuana."

Johnston starts to say something but Klein slams the trunk closed. He gets in the car placing the brown paper bag on the seat beside him. He starts the engine and heads back to Los Angeles. He taps the hands-free phone button on the steering wheel. It rings.

Freddie King: "King Bail Bonds, Freddie King, King of the bail bond's business."
Jake Klein: "It's me. I got him."
Freddie King: "Great, where is he?"
Jake Klein: "He's in the trunk."
Freddie King: "The trunk! Jesus Jake, I need him back alive."
Jake Klein: "You should have mentioned that before…"
Freddie King: "Jake…"
Jake Klein: "Don't worry Freddie, I'll get him in the back seat as soon as I get out of town and find some back road where he won't give me any trouble."

Klein hangs up before Freddie can bitch any more about his tactics.

DATE NIGHT

Outside the Forest Arms Condominium,
Woodland Hills, Los Angeles

An attractive dark haired woman, Joanne Leslie, anxiously waits in her car watching the lobby entrance of the Forest Arms condominium in the Woodland Hills district of Los Angeles.

She takes a small yellow previously used prescription container out of her jacket pocket. She dabs a small amount of cocaine onto the back of her hand. She snorts the white powder; she wipes the residue from her nose and settles back to wait.

Forest Arms Condominium, Allie Ness's suite.

Inside on the second floor in Suite 503 Allie Ness and Donald Davis untangle themselves from a white leather Bauhaus couch. The couple rearrange their clothing while Allie pours the last bit of red wine into the two long-stemmed glasses that have been neglected for the last half hour of horizontal *Batachata.*

Davis: "I've got to go."
Ness: "But we haven't even crossed the finish line coach."
Davis: "Yeah, tell me about it, but I got to get back. I have an early day to tomorrow."
Ness: "You sure?"
Davis: "I want to stay but I can't. I still have to do some last-minute prep for tomorrow's meeting."

Davis is searching around for his car keys, looking in the

pockets of the charcoal gray cashmere sports jacket he haphazardly tossed on the white Marcel Breuer armchair.

Ness: "You tossed them on the desk when we came in."

Davis walks over to the minimalist silver tubular desk with the black leather top. He looks down and spots his keys.

Directly behind the car keys is a silver-framed photograph of Ness kissing the cheek of the attractive dark haired woman impatiently waiting in her car outside. He picks up the frame.

Davis: "Who this?"
Ness: "Jealous?"
Davis: "Should I be?"

Ness ignores the question.

Ness: "I thought you were in a hurry to leave?"
Davis: "Yeah, I've got to get moving."

Not wanting to leave things up in the air.

Ness: "She's an old friend from college. We get together a couple times a year and bitch about life."
Davis: "Seem kind of close."
Ness: "College you know… experimenting with things… all kinds of things."
Davis: "I bet. You'll have to tell me about her but not tonight."

Davis puts on his jacket, bends down and kisses Ness. "I'm sorry about the money. It's just not a good time."

Ness: "Don't worry about it. You can bring me sandwiches when they put me in debtor's prison."
Davis: "I'm pretty sure they don't do that anymore… they just send you to a work farm. You'd look cute in those Daisy Mae cut-offs."
Ness: "Very funny."
Davis: "Got to run. I'll pop by after work tomorrow and we'll do it up right."

Davis leaves. A few minutes later the lobby buzzer sounds.

Ness: "Yes, who is it?"
Leslie: "It's me."

Ness presses the button to let the attractive dark haired woman enter the building. A few minutes later there's a knock. Ness opens the door. Joanne Leslie grabs Ness by the hair on the back of her head. She looks Ness right in the eye. Their heads are only inches apart. She kisses Ness passionately on the mouth.

Ness: "Well… hello to you too."

Leslie walks in without replying. She takes off her Donna Karan jacket and tosses it on the Breuer armchair.

Ness: "I guess nobody uses a closet anymore."
Leslie ignores her, "Did he give you the money?"
Ness: "No. He says it's not a good time."
Leslie: "I told you I need that money."
Ness: "Well, I guess you're going to have to get it someplace else. Maybe if you cut back on the Donna Karan and Vera Wang, you wouldn't need the money."

Leslie forces herself to calm down. The only reason she puts up with Ness, the uptown bitch with the downtown tastes, is to get her hands on the money. She approaches Ness, puts a hand gently on her cheek and kisses her again.

Leslie: "To hell with the money, let's go to bed."

THE SURPRISE

Outside the door of Allie Ness's suite.

The following day, as promised, Davis arrives at the front door of Ness's apartment with a bottle of Bollinger Brut and an attaché case filled with five thousand dollars. He uses his key to unlock the door and enter.

He looks around but Allie isn't in the living room. He figures she's still in the bedroom getting ready. He tosses his jacket on the Breuer and places the attaché case on the desk.

Davis: "I hope you're still not sore about last night. Anyway… I got a surprise for you."

He goes to the bar and uncorks the champagne with a large pop! He grabs a couple of long-stemmed glasses and pours the champagne.

Davis: "Guess what Baby? I got you the dough you needed."

With the Bollinger Brut in one hand and the two glasses of champagne in the other he enters Allie's bedroom. Ness isn't there.

Disappointed, Davis puts the champagne down on the nightstand; he slips off his black soft as butter Italian loafers and lies down on Allie's bed to wait for her.

The next morning he wakes up to find he's alone on the bed still wearing his clothes. He gets up and goes into the kitchen expecting to see Allie making breakfast. She's not there. Davis is concerned… but first he needs to use the facilities. He goes into Allie's bathroom en suite and notices the shower curtain is pulled shut. It's something Allie never does, concerned that mould will form on the tiles. He pushes back the curtain and looks down. Allie's naked body is sprawled across the oversized Jacuzzi bathtub.

Davis: "Jesus Christ!"

Davis, shaking, tears welling up in the corner of his eyes walks unsteadily into the bedroom. He sits down on the bed gathering his thoughts. He picks up the bedside phone and dials the police.

Police: "Los Angeles Police Department, Woodland Hills Division, how can I direct your call?"

Davis: "I'd like to report a murder…"

THE GOLD CRICKET

The Lockup Cop Bar

The Lockup is your standard LA cop bar complete with pictures of distinguished local heroes killed in action hanging on the sandblasted brick walls. The tables are worn mahogany surrounded by matching wooden chairs all of which have suffered under the abuse of the heavy drinking men in blue and their groupie acquaintances.

The floor is littered with discarded peanut shells providing a weird crunching sound barely audible over the raucous din of oversized men letting off some steam. It's a place Klein is comfortable frequenting, both for the company, provided by attractive women who mistake him for a senior detective, and for the odd bit of information he picks up from eavesdropping on drunken loose-mouth conversations.

Klein notices Detective Matt Caplinski walk in and waves for him to come over. Caplinski heads to Klein's table and takes a seat.

Caplinski: "I hear you brought in our old pal Cheesy."
Klein: "I told you I would."
Caplinski: "I guess you saved Freddie a bundle?"
Klein: "Ain't that the truth. Freddie was sweating like a prized pig at a Texas barbeque."
Caplinski: "Tell me… do the ladies fall for that down-home act of yours."
Klein: "I like to think I'm flexible. I move with whatever the situation calls for."

Caplinski: "Well I bet they like the flexible part at least."

Caplinski starts to get up to join his cop buddies.

Klein: "Where are you running? There's a small matter of settling our wager. Something about, 'I'll bet you $50 bucks you can't bring that sack of shit, Cheesy Johnston, in before his court date.' You remember that conversation don't you?"

Caplinski sits back down frustrated by his attempt at getting away clean.

Caplinski: "You really going to hold me to that bet? I was hammered when I said that…"
Klein: "A bet's a bet, besides… you weren't that hammered, and I don't have a government pension to fall back on in my fast approaching declining years."

Caplinski reaches into his pocket and pulls out a roll of cash. He peels off five ten-dollar bills and places them on the table. Klein takes out his gold money clip with the embossed cricket and carefully slides the five tens into place.

Caplinski: "What drug dealer did you take that little gem away from?"

Klein holds up the money clip admiringly…

Klein: "I actually buy my shit. I don't have access to the police evidence room to pick out little knick-knacks."

Caplinski: "Fuck you too Klein. Remind me to never get drunk with you again. I can't afford the fallout."

Caplinski gets up and leaves. An attractive dark haired woman in tight designer jeans, a white cotton Vera Wang shirt unbuttoned just enough to 'say hello to my little friends,' and a Donna Karan black leather jacket approaches Klein's table.

Leslie: "Is this seat taken?"

ONE NIGHT STAND

Klein's Apartment Bedroom

Klein is asleep in bed with Leslie beside him. Her cell phone vibrates. Klein still asleep stirs… Leslie reaches for the phone and answers it.

Leslie: "Yeah… what's up? Okay I got it, I'll be right there."

Leslie slides her naked body out of bed to retrieve her clothes.

Klein: "Is everything all right?"

Leslie dresses quickly.

Leslie: "Yeah, I just got to go to work. Some emergency."
Klein: "I never got your name?"
Leslie: "I'll leave it and my number on your desk. Go back to sleep."

Klein rolls over and goes back to sleep. Leslie goes to Klein's desk in the far corner of the room located under the window that overlooks the street below. She opens the top drawer to see if she can find a pen and paper to write on. She spots Klein's gold money clip with the embossed cricket.

She closes the drawer and opens the file drawer underneath. The files have all been pushed back against the back of the drawer to make room for a brown paper bag filled with cash. Leslie stops and stares, taking in the prize. Just what she needs to get herself out of a jam.

She turns and looks at Klein making sure he's still asleep. He's out like a light, not surprising based on the animated previous few hours of cardio.

Leslie carefully pulls the brown bag out of the file drawer trying desperately not to alert Klein with the crumbling sound of the paper bag. As she pulls the bag from the drawer she looks back over her shoulder making sure Klein doesn't wake up.

With the bag safely extracted from it's not too safe hiding place, Leslie turns to leave, but stops. She turns back to the desk and reopens the top drawer. She looks down at the gold cricket money clip holding at least a couple hundred dollars. She spots a box of tissues on the desk. She gently pulls out a tissue from the box and carefully lifts the clip out of the drawer making sure her fingers don't touch the metal.

She slips the money out of the clip trying to decide whether to just take the money, the clip, or both.

Leslie: "Fuck it!"

She slips the money back into the money clip still wrapped in the tissue and slides it into her tight designer jeans. She goes to the door and leaves.

THE CRIME SCENE

Outside Allie Ness's Condo

Leslie pulls up and parks her restored 1963 fire engine red Austin Healey with black leather interior in front of the two parked police cruisers. A uniformed cop, Bill Anderson, approaches Leslie as she gets out of the convertible.

Billy: "Nice wheels."
Leslie: "Someday Billy when you grow up and become a big bad detective like me, you too can drive in style."

Billy points to Davis sitting in the back seat of his cruiser.

Billy: "It was called in by the boyfriend, Donald Davis, a lawyer. I put him in the back of my cruiser figuring he's suspect one. Leslie looks over at Davis in the back of the cop car."
Leslie: "See that Billy-boy you're on your way to a gold shield already."
Billy: "Freddy is guarding the door to the condo… No. 503. Once we saw the body, we hustled him out of there before any evidence got fucked up."
Leslie: "Where's Harry?"
Billy: "Dispatch said your partner would be late. He had to call his Ex to see if she could take the kids."

Leslie walks over to Billy's cruiser and looks in the window. She opens the door to speak with Davis. Davis looks at her strangely almost as if he recognizes her.

Davis: "You look familiar, are you a friend of Allie's."

Davis pushes back her black leather Donna Karan jacket revealing her gold shield and a Glock G43 9mm pistol, tightly held in place by a black leather shoulder holster.

Davis: "Sorry… I thought we might have met before. I'm still pretty shaken up."
Leslie: "Where did you find the body?"
Davis: "In the bath tube."
Leslie: "What were you doing in the bathroom?"

Davis a little confused by the question.

Davis: "I had to take a leak."
Leslie: "You just walked into the bathroom and saw the body?"
Davis: "Not exactly…"
Leslie: "Well why don't you tell me, exactly."
Davis: "The shower curtain was drawn closed."
Leslie: "You always go around rearranging your girlfriend's stuff?"

Davis, getting increasing nervous and flustered by the questions, "No, of course not, it's just that…"
Leslie: "It's just that what?"
Davis: "Allie never leaves the shower curtain drawn closed. She's paranoid about mould."

Leslie gives Davis a hard stare for no other reason than to keep him on the defensive. The more defensive he appears, the guiltier he'll look to her colleagues that always focus on the boyfriend or husband.

Leslie: "I see… a bit OCD was she?"

Davis: "No, not really, she just..."
Leslie doesn't wait for a response. "One of these fine police officers will take you downtown so you can make a statement."

She closes the cruiser door and walks back to Billy.

Leslie: "Call dispatch and tell them you're bringing the boyfriend in for questioning. Have them call Harry and have him go directly to the station so he can interview the boyfriend while I take care of the crime scene. Are the techs on their way?"
Billy: "I figured you'd want to look around first."
Leslie: "Good thinking. I'll take a quick look around while I wait for them."

Billy heads for his car to take Davis in while Leslie heads up to Allie Ness's condo.

Davis steps out of the elevator and heads to apartment 503. A uniformed cop, Freddy Gomez, Billy's partner, stands guard outside.

Leslie: "Anybody try to get in?"
Freddy: "No Sir, err Ma'am..."
Leslie: "You and Billy nose-around to see if there was anything you like?
Freddy: "No Ma'am! We wouldn't do anything like that."
Leslie: "You sure?"
Freddy: "Yes Ma'am! As soon as the boyfriend showed us the body, we got him and ourselves out of there P.D.Q."
Leslie: "Okay, good."

Leslie opens the door and enters the familiar condo of her deceased sometime girlfriend Allie Ness. Leslie goes straight to the bathroom. She dispassionately views her deceased lover sprawled across the Jacuzzi tube.

She leaves the bathroom and heads for the bedroom where she notices the rumbled bedcovers. Davis must not have realized Ness was stashed in the Jacuzzi; figuring she was out, he falls asleep waiting for her. Of course the rumbled bedspread could also be seen by her fellow men in blue as the sign of a struggle.

Leslie thinks, "Jesus men are stupid. They'll always jump to the quickest solution. Throw the fucker in the slammer whether he's guilty or not. Move on to the next piece of shit that finds himself in the wrong place at the wrong time. And that's the beauty of the whole plan."

Leslie analyses the scene with the practiced eye of a seasoned homicide cop. She reaches into her pocket and pulls out the tissue wrapped gold money clip with the embossed cricket. She removes most of the money leaving fifty bucks in the clip for the sake of credibility. She drops the clip on the floor nudging it part way under the bedspread with her foot. The crime scene techs would have to be blind to miss it.

She then heads back into the living room to see if there is anything in the room that could lead to anyone tying her to Ness. She takes a quick tour around the room and ends up by the minimalist tubular desk with the black leather top. Leslie spots the brief case and the silver picture frame.

Leslie: "Shit... The fucking picture."

She picks up the frame, but she has no place to put. She looks around but can't think of anyplace to hide it. She absentmindedly opens the brief case to see what's in it.

Leslie: "Jackpot!"

Leslie looks intently at the contents as if it was silently saying take me I'm yours. Five thousand dollars neatly arranged in neat stacks leaving just enough room for her to stash the picture frame. She closes the attaché case leaving it on the desk. She goes to the front door and opens it.

Leslie: "Freddy... I forgot my phone, go down to my car and get it for me... I tossed it on the passenger seat."
Freddy: "Clancy's downstairs watching the lobby, I'll call down and have him bring it up."
Leslie: "What the fuck is it with you guys? Did anyone tell you to think! Clancy guards the fucking lobby and you do what the fuck I tell you to. Now get me my fucking phone before I decide to write you up for insubordination."
Freddy: "Okay, okay, I'm going..."

Freddy starts down the hallway mumbling to himself.

Freddy: "Bitch must be on the rag or something."
Leslie still standing in the doorway watching him. "I can fucking hear you asshole!"

An elderly man and woman in a neighboring apartment stick their heads out their front door to see what the ruckus is all about. Leslie turns to look at them...

Leslie: "Police business! Get back inside!"

The elderly woman starts to say something, but her husband stops her, gently pushing her back inside their apartment. Leslie goes back inside and grabs the attaché case. She quickly walks down the hall turning right just after the elevator. She opens a door to a small room that contains a garbage shoot and a recycle bin. She hides the attaché case behind the recycle bin. She heads back to Ness's apartment just in time for Freddy's return.

Freddy: "Your phone wasn't there."
Leslie: "Yeah, okay… I found it in my jacket pocket."

Freddy doesn't say a word. He knows better than to start up with a detective, especially this woman detective. A few minutes later three crime scene techs show up carrying all their nerd paraphernalia.

Crime Scene Tech: "Evening Detective… Where's the body?"
Leslie: "She's in the bathroom. I'll get out of your way so you can do your thing. Make sure you collect all the evidence. And check the bedroom carefully, the bed shows signs of a struggle."

Leslie leaves the apartment but as she leaves, she gives Freddy a half-ass apology. "Freddy… sorry about earlier, it's late and I'm a little testy."
Freddy: "A little testy?"
Leslie: "Don't push it pal. Now go in and see if the crime scene nerds need any help."
Freddy: "Since when do they need my help?"
Leslie: "Can't you just do what the fuck you're told?"

Freddy shrugs and goes inside knowing full well the crime nerds will tell him to get the hell out before he contaminates the scene.

Meanwhile Leslie quickly retrieves the attaché case before hustling down the five flights of back stairs and out the garage door. She gets back to her car, opens the trunk, and tosses the attaché case in beside Jake Klein's brown paper bag of money. She gets in the driver's seat and enters a number on her cell phone.

Leslie: "Hi it's me. It's done. We're square… now fuck off.
Cheesy: "Oh baby, we're hardly done. Getting rid of the witness was only the vig. There's still the matter of principal that needs to be cleared up."
Leslie: "You better keep in mind I'm a cop!"
Cheesy: "Honey, I'm well aware of what kind of cop you are. That's what makes our arrangement so… simpatico."
Leslie: "Fuck off Cheesy."
Cheesy: "Be nice baby… you know I prefer Clarence."
Leslie: "My mistake… Fuck Off Clarence!

And she hangs up.

CLARENCE, MY OLD PAL

The Lockup Cop Bar

Klein sits at the back of The Lockup with a clear view of everybody that walks into the bar, hoping the bitch with the great body and his five grand comes back for seconds. He's pissed, it wasn't just the money; she took the gold cricket money clip as well.

Chessy's 5G's was a nice score, something to put away for a rainy day. Five grand is tempting for anybody on the make but why the hell did she have to take the money clip. It was his rabbit's foot, his good luck charm.

An old Chinese gentleman, Mr. Chen, gave it to him when he helped his son out of a jam. It was a nice thing to do, and the old man told him it would bring him good luck, and it had. He could understand the bitch taking the money; she had to pay for those fancy threads somehow; but why take the money clip. She could have taken the money from the clip and left the clip but no, the bitch had to take the money clip too.

Klein: "What's the matter with people today?"

A copy of the LA Evening Star slams down on the table almost knocking over Klein's Boston Sour. A lone skinny finger with a skull and crossbones ring points to a small article at the bottom of the page under a mug shot of Clarence 'Cheesy' Johnston.

D.A. Drops Case Against Clarence 'Cheesy' Johnston
Eye Witness Allie Ness Found Murdered In Her Luxury Condo

Klein looks up to see Cheesy looming menacingly over him.

Cheesy: "Mr. Smith, I presume?"
Klein: "Evening Clarence. I suppose congratulations are in order?"
Cheesy remains standing, "I prefer to discuss the small matter of five thousand dollars paid in good faith for services not rendered."
Klein: "About that money... I'd love to return it but... well... I met this young lady and..."
Cheesy: "Bring me my fucking money or witnesses won't be the only ones that turn up dead." Cheesy turns and heads for the door.

Parking Lot of The Lockup Cop Bar

Cheesy exits The Lockup just as Joanne Leslie pulls up in her classic red Austin Healey. She gets out of the sports car not noticing Cheesy coming towards her. He grabs her by the arm and schleps her towards his white Cadillac Escalade. He pushes her hard up against the side of the car. His body is pressed tight against her; he has her by the wrists so she can't get at her piece. His face is only inches away from hers.

Leslie: "You know, you really should get laid more often; it might curb some of your more violent tendencies."
Cheesy: "You're one to talk."
Leslie: "If you want to fuck, all you have to do is ask. No need for the rough stuff."

Cheesy still has her pinned up against the side of the Cadillac. He can feel Leslie's hips pushing up against him in an effort to avoid the inevitable.

Cheesy: "You got my money?"
Leslie: "No I ain't got your money, and even if I did, I wouldn't fucking give it to you."
Cheesy: "Is that so?"
Leslie: "Yeah, that's so… I paid my debt. Knocking-off witnesses is an expensive ask. In fact, I think a lifetime supply of powder would be fair compensation."
Cheesy: "Is that what you think?"
Leslie: "Listen asshole, I'm still a cop, and no one would give a shit if I put a hole in your fucking head right here in the parking lot."

Cheesy releases her wrists and takes a step back.

Cheesy: "You better watch yourself sweetheart, even cops aren't bullet proof." Leslie walks back to her car.
Cheesy: "Thought you were going in for a drink?"
Leslie: "Lost my appetite."

She gets into her car and drives off. Cheesy watches her pull out of the parking lot. He turns to see Jake Klein standing just outside the bar door watching. Cheesy waves to Klein to come over. Klein walks to where Cheesy is standing.

Cheesy: "Get in. We need to talk."

Klein opens the passenger door and gets in; Cheesy walks around the other side and gets in the driver's side.

Klein: "We going for a ride?"
Cheesy: "You better hope we're not? Besides, I like you, and you owe me a favor."

Klein: "If you like me so much how come you threatened to kill me a few minutes ago."

Cheesy: "Situations are always in flux."

Klein: "Jesus, Clarence, you're deep, kind of the Spinoza of drug dealers."

Cheesy: "Spin-who? He some kind of cartel boss or something?"

Klein: "Yeah, or something..."

Cheesy: "Listen I get it. We all have a job to do. It's how things work, but you fucked up, and there're consequences."

Klein: "So you told me."

Cheesy: "You say you don't have my money, okay... some broad stole it, or you lost it at the track, or you shoved it up your nose, I really don't give a shit. The bottom line is you owe me."

Klein: "Okay, Clarence, I'll play. What do you want?"

Cheesy: "You're not the only one who owes me money, there's this broad..."

Cheesy prattles on about the bitch cop that owes him money, the same bitch that screwed Klein, both literally and figuratively. Klein recognized her from across the parking lot when Cheesy had her pinned to the side of the Escalade. But now he knew she was a cop, and that made things harder.

Klein: "I get your money... we're square?"

Cheesy: "Yeah that's what I've been saying."

Klein: "Okay Clarence, we got a deal, but this could take some time."

Cheesy: "Yeah well, don't take too long, or I may have to charge you a penalty." Klein opens the car door but Cheesy grabs him by the arm.

Cheesy: "If she happens to disappear altogether, maybe I come up with a bonus." Klein doesn't bother answering. He just leaves.

THE GIRL IN THE SILVER FRAME

Police Station, Interrogation Room

Detective Harry Marshall, Leslie's partner, sits across the table from Donald Davis in the interrogation room.

Davis: "Look I just came in today to see about my money. I already gave you my statement a couple of days ago. Stop asking me the same damn questions... I fell asleep waiting for Allie and when I got up to take a leak, I found her in the bathroom."

Leslie enters and positions herself in the corner of the room barely lit by the single sixty-watt fixture hanging from the ceiling. Marshall turns to Leslie.

Marshall: "He keeps going on about five thousand dollars he left in the apartment."
Leslie: "Ask the crime scene boys. Don't ask me. They're the ones that collected all the evidence."
Davis: "It was in an attaché case on the desk, right next to a picture of Allie and her friend."

Leslie takes a step closer to the light. "I didn't see any attaché case or photograph."
Davis: "Hay, aren't you the woman in the picture kissing Allie, her friend from college? I thought I recognized you."
Marshall turns to Leslie. "You know what the fuck he's talking about?"
Leslie: "I haven't clue."

Davis leans in closer to Marshall "I'm telling you, I left five thousand dollars in a leather attaché case on the desk beside a picture of Allie kissing your partner."
Leslie: "Not only is this asshole guilty, he's delusional."

Marshall gets up and goes to the door and opens it. Detective Matt Caplinski is sitting at his desk drinking coffee.

Marshall: "Matt, go down to the evidence room and bring up the box of stuff the nerds collected for the Ness case."
Marshall turns back to Davis. "If your phantom money and picture were there, the nerds would have collected it."

Five minutes later Caplinski knocks on the interrogation room door. Leslie opens the door.

Caplinski: "The stuff's on my desk."

Leslie and Marshall start to leave. Davis gets up to follow.

Leslie turns to look at Davis. "Where do you think you're going? Sit-the-fuck-down and wait!"

Davis, frustrated sits down with a thump. Leslie and Marshall walk to Caplinski's desk. Leslie looks at Caplinski.

Leslie: "It's your desk, be my guest."

Caplinski opens the box... he's stunned. Staring him in the face on top of all the other stuff is an evidence bag containing a gold money clip with an embossed cricket.

Leslie: "You see an attaché case?"

Marshall: "Nope!"

Leslie pulls the evidence bags out of the box and lays them out on the desk. Caplinski can't take his eyes off the money clip.

Leslie: "You see a silver frame with me kissing anybody?"
Marshall looks at Leslie. "Who said anything about a silver picture frame?"

Caplinski looks up at Leslie.

Leslie: "Look at the apartment for Christ's sake. Everything is silver and chrome. You think this dame would just tape the photo to her expensive black leather desk?"

Caplinski walks over to the interrogation room and opens the door.

Davis: "You find the money?"
Caplinski ignores the question. "Was the photo just lying on the desk?"
Davis: "No... it was in a nice silver frame."

Caplinski looks back at Marshall, then at Leslie.

Leslie: "Jesus... I confess, I read Architectural Digest."

Caplinski and Marshall smile.

WHERE'S MY MONEY?

The Lockup Cop Bar

Donald Davis enters The Lockup and goes straight to the bar. He orders a drink and asks the bartender a question. The bartender shakes his head and starts to walk away but Davis stops him. Davis places two twenties on the bar. The bartender points to a table in the back and pockets the cash. Davis takes his drink and walks directly to where the barkeep pointed.

Davis: "Excuse me. Are you Jake Klein?" Klein looks up from his drink.
Klein: "That depends. Who's asking?" Davis sits down across from Klein.
Klein: "Have a seat, why don't you?"
Davis: "I'm Donald Davis, a lawyer and I need your help."
Klein: "Look, if one of your clients skipped bail, you'll have to call the office." Klein reaches into his pocket and pulls out a business card. He slides it across the table to Davis.
Klein: "Ask for Freddie."
Davis: "No it's nothing like that. My girlfriend was murdered, perhaps you heard about it: Allie Ness, it's all over the papers."
Klein: "Sure I heard about it, but that's a police matter."
Davis: "There's something fishy going on."
Klein: "What do you mean, fishy?"
Davis: "Allie needed some money… five thousand dollars…"
Klein: "For what?"
Davis: "I didn't ask. She said it was to pay some debts, but I think it was for a friend."
Klein: "Go on…"

Davis: "Anyway, I told her it was a bad time but then I collected from a client I thought was going to stiff me, so I thought we would celebrate. I went over to her place with the cash and some champagne, but she wasn't home, or at least that's what I thought. She was stashed in the bathtub."

Klein: "I don't understand what any of this has to do with me."

Davis: "The cops say the money wasn't there. And that's bullshit. It was in the attaché case on the desk when they showed up and hustled me out into a squad car like I was the murderer."

Klein: "The attaché case was just sitting on the desk."

Davis: "Yes… right beside the photograph of Allie kissing this female detective."

Klein: "What female detective?"

Davis: "Her name's Leslie, and that's another thing, the photo was also missing. The whole thing stinks."

Klein: "This female cop, you say her name was Leslie?"

Davis: "Yeah, I'm positive."

Klein: "Nice looking, dark hair, great body, and expensive threads?"

Davis: "That's the bitch."

Klein: "Yeah… that's the bitch all right."

Davis: "Something else strange happened."

Klein: "I bet."

Davis: "This other detective, Matt something, went to get the evidence box to check for the money and photo of Allie.

Klein: "Matt Caplinski?"

Davis: "Could be… anyway he comes back and starts asking me if the photo was in a frame, what the hell else would it be in? Look, they want to pin this thing on me and I've got nothing to do with it, besides I want my money back. You get the money back and find out what the hell is going on and I'll give you half, twenty-five hundred."

Klein thinks for a moment, this whole thing is getting complicated. "I'll nose around and see what I can find out. How do I get in touch?"

Davis takes a leather business card holder out of his pocket and hands Klein one of his cards.

Davis: "Let me know as soon as you find anything out."

The two men shake hands and Davis leaves. Klein stares at the ice cube in his drink as if it was a shaman's rune hiding the key to understanding what exactly was going on.

The bitch cop with the sticky fingers was at it again. And the whole business with the picture frame was weird, she was obviously bent, so he could understand her taking the money, but why the picture frame, why the money clip, unless she had something to do with Ness's murder. With this bitch anything was possible.

Klein's concentration is broken by Matt Caplinski depositing his cop-sized bulk down in the chair previously occupied by Donald Davis.

Caplinski: "Let me see your fancy money clip?"
Klein: "What?"
Caplinski: "Let me see your god damn money clip now!"
Klein: "It was stolen."
Caplinski: "Of all the people, Klein, you're the last one I would think would knock-off a civilian."
Klein: "What the hell are you talking about?"
Caplinski: "We found your missing money clip under Allie Ness's bed where you dropped it during the struggle."

Klein: "You're nuts! Your colleague Detective Leslie, stole it, along with the five thousand bucks Cheesy gave me to get him out of the country."
Caplinski: "But you brought him in?"
Klein: "Yah, I'm guilty of lying to a drug dealer in order to bring him in for trial."
Caplinski: "How do you know Leslie stole the clip?"
Klein: "Well let's see… we were lying in bed after fucking each other's brains out, her phone buzzes, and she says she has to take off. I didn't know she was a cop, I fell sleep, and she fucking robs me."

Caplinski is quiet for a moment. "Ness's boyfriend kept going on about some missing money from the crime scene, and a photo of Leslie kissing Ness."
Klein: "Who was first on the scene?"
Caplinski: "According to the file, a couple of uniforms got there first, put Davis in a cruiser, and waited for Leslie."
Klein: "That must have been the call she got at my place. What about her partner?"
Caplinski: "He went to the station to interview Davis while Leslie checked the crime scene… Shit!"
Klein: "Alone? Before the crime scene guys showed up?"
Caplinski: "Yah… son-of-a-bitch."

OLD FRIENDS

Beverly Center, Miracle Mile

Klein pulls up to the gate of a two story Spanish Colonial complete with tile roof and stucco exterior. He presses the speaker hanging on the gatepost. It crackles to life.

Voice: "Yeah… what do you want?"
Klein: "Jake Klein to see Clarence."

The speaker box buzzes and crackles before to falls back to sleep. The rustic ornate Spanish inspired wrought-iron gate opens allowing Klein to enter the mini estate. He pulls up to the front door.

A very large athletic black man in cream-colored trousers and a black cotton polo shirt stretched to its limit comes out to greet Klein. Hanging precariously from a black leather shoulder holster is a .50 caliber brushed chrome Desert Eagle. The man approaches Klein with open arms as Klein exits his car.

Klein: "Jesus Christ is that you, Tiny?"

He grabs Klein in a bear hug almost cracking two ribs. "God damn right it's me. How the fuck are you?"

Klein: "Can't complain. You're looking prosperous?"
Tiny: "You mean fat?"
Klein: "Is there a difference?"
Tiny: "Jeez it's good to see you. How long has it been… ten years?"
Klein: "Fifteen, Winter Ball in the Dominican I think."

Tiny: "Boy those were the days. Fun, sun, and broads, I miss it."
Klein: "Jesus, what the hell are you doing here? And that fucking cannon you got hanging from your shoulder, what's up with that?"
Tiny: "Not a lot of work for has-been ball players, so I take what I can get. And this prick needs an intimidator."
Klein: "You should put that on a business card, "Tiny Wilson, The Intimidator, Have Cannon Will Travel." Both men smile.
Tiny: "I like the sound of it, "The Intimidator"… I just might do that. So you got business with this asshole? I hope you're not using."
Klein: "Nah, nothing like that. My partying days are done, but listen, something's going down, and Cheesy's going down with it. So maybe pack up your cannon and find another gig."
Tiny: "Not that many people looking to hire a black Paladin to stand around and look scary." Klein takes a business card from his pocket and hands it to Tiny.
Klein: "Go speak to Freddie, tell him I said to hire you. We can always use someone with your talents."
Tiny; "Bounty Hunter, ah? Shit, that could work."
Klein: "Where do I find your boss?"
Tiny: "I'll take you around the back."

Klein and Tiny reminisce about the good old days as they take the patterned concrete path to the backyard, dominated by a large swimming pool.

Lounging in a chaise beside a beautiful almost naked blonde is Clarence "Cheesy" Johnston wrapped in a hideous, brightly colored beach towel but still wearing his signature black leather embossed cowboy hat.

Tiny: "You got a visitor boss."

Cheesy looks up from the concoction of fruit and alcohol that he's nursing, tips back his black Stetson, and smiles.

Klein: "Clarence…"
Cheesy: "Take a load off."

Cheesy waves for Klein to sit in the chair beside him. Tiny stands off to the side waiting for instructions.

Cheesy: "You bring my money?"
Klein: "Nope, something better."
Cheesy: "Ain't nothing better than money my friend, except maybe pussy, and without money, there ain't no pussy."

Klein looks around the backyard. The back of the house is all glass revealing Cheesy's bedroom en suite shower with another of Cheesy's stable of female friends enjoying a long hot shower.

Klein: "Nice place you got here. Great view."
Cheesy slaps the butt of the almost naked blonde beside him. "Why don't you go help Tanya lather up."

The blonde gets up, kisses Cheesy on the cheek, and heads for the shower to join Tanya.

Cheesy: "So what's better than money?"
Klein: "Information."
Cheesy: "Let's have it; it's almost time for my afternoon siesta."
Klein: "Your cop friend has your money; in fact, she literally has your money. She's the one that stole the money from my apartment."
Cheesy: "Why didn't you tell me this before?"

Klein: "I didn't know who she was, or that she had anything to do with you. I didn't even know she was a cop.
Cheesy: "Yah, and I bet you didn't know she was the one that knocked off Ness."
Klein: "I figured it was something like that."
Cheesy: "Okay fine. Go get my money and get rid of her while you're at it."
Klein: "Not a chance, Clarence. I'm not killing anybody. I brought you the information so you go get your money yourself."
Cheesy: "You know my man here used to be a pretty good ball player, like you, only he could hit. And he still has his bats handy in case people don't do as I ask."
Klein: "Like I said I have information that may change your mind."
Cheesy: "I'll be the judge of that."
Klein: "I'm guessing our cop friend owed you the money, and you got her to knock off Ness as payment."
Cheesy: "So what?"
Klein: "Leslie and Ness were old pals, pretty close from what I gather. So Ness was supposed to get the money from her boyfriend."
Cheesy: "Old news my friend, tell me something I don't know."
Klein: "The night Leslie killed Ness, the boyfriend showed up with the cash, and since Leslie was the first detective to arrive on the scene, she grabbed the money. The bitch is sitting on ten grand."
Cheesy: "I knew I couldn't trust that bitch. Okay Jake, we're square, now get lost. And I don't have to remind you to forget this whole arrangement, *capisce*?
Klein: "Clarence, it's already forgotten."
Cheesy: "Tiny... show our friend out."

Tiny and Klein walk to the front of the house.

Klein: "Listen Tiny, this whole thing is going sideways. I'm telling you as a friend, get lost before the shit hits the fan. You do not want to get caught holding the bag for that piece of dreck."

Tiny: "I don't know if I can. I'm already in pretty deep. He's going to want me to do the dirty work."

Klein: "Okay listen, I got an idea. Hold tight and stall till I get back to you."

Tiny scribbles his cell phone number on one of Jake's cards, and hands it to Klein. The men shake hands and Klein leaves.

A CHEESY PLAN

Joanne Leslie's Apartment Building

Jake Klein pulls up in front of Leslie's apartment building and parks behind her red Austin Healey sports car. He gets out of his car and approaches the doorman.

Doorman: "Good Evening Sir, who are you here to visit?"
Klein: "Joanne Leslie."

The Doorman reaches to push the button to announce Klein's arrival but stops. "Who shall I say is here?"

Klein takes a wade of cash out of his pocket and peels off a twenty-dollar bill. "It's a surprise."

The Doorman looks at the twenty and then at Klein. "What kind of surprise?"

Klein peels off another twenty from his roll. "A big surprise."

The Doorman takes both twenties and opens the lobby door. "Apartment 408… but being an old friend you already knew that."

Klein enters the lobby and heads for the elevator.

Leslie has two rails of cocaine neatly laid out on her glass coffee table beside a laptop computer playing a rerun of *Dexter*. Her spare Glock sits on the table close at hand. She uses a tightly wrapped twenty-dollar bill to snort the two lines of cocaine, one after another.

Her small but elegant Echo Park apartment is well furnished, dominated by a large black leather couch facing the window that overlooks the street below. Two matching oversized black leather chairs flank the couch. There's a knock on the door. She grabs the piece and stuffs it behind the cushions of the couch. She crosses the room to answer the door. She opens it.

Klein: "Hello again."
Leslie is surprised to see him. "You… How'd you find me?"

Klein pushes his way past her and takes a seat in the middle of the couch in front of the computer. Klein looks down at the computer to see *Dexter* doing his handiwork. He looks up at Leslie who is standing over him, her hands on her hips.

Klein: "Getting pointers?"
Leslie: "How'd you find me?"
Klein: "It's kind of my job, finding people."
Leslie: "What do you want?"
Klein: "You didn't leave me your number."
Leslie: "I guess I forgot. You weren't really worth remembering."
Klein: "Ouch! That's kind of cruel don't you think, after all we meant to each other."
Leslie: "Do you mind? I'm missing my program."
Klein: "I think we have business to discuss."
Leslie: "Yeah, business… what kind of business?"
Klein: "Five thousand dollar business, and the matter of a gold cricket money clip." There's a knock on the door.
Leslie: "Jesus Christ! Where the hell's the doorman?" She starts to answer the door but Klein stops her.
Klein: "Ah… don't bother, I'll get it, it's for me anyway."

Klein goes to the door and opens it. It's Matt Caplinski.

Caplinski: "Any trouble?"
Klein: "Not so far."

Caplinski enters the apartment. Leslie is surprised.

Leslie: "You two clowns know each other?"
Caplinski: "Oh yah, we're old pals from way back."
Leslie: "So what's the deal here?"

Both men take seats on the couch. Leslie remains standing, nervously weighing her untenable options, like an antelope singled out from the herd.

Caplinski: "Is that *Dexter*? I love that show."

Caplinski looks at the glass coffee table and spots the cocaine residue beside the computer. He licks his finger, sticks it in the residue and touches it to his tongue. He looks up at Leslie.

Caplinski: Dinner?" She doesn't answer.
Caplinski: "My friend here doesn't like woman that fuck and run, especially when they take off with his stuff."
Leslie: "What's that got to do with you, that's between him and me?"
Caplinski: "Me, oh I'm more interested in the reason you tried to frame him by planting his rather unusual gold money clip."

There's a knock on the door.

Leslie: "Now what for god's sake?"
Klein: "I forgot to mention, Cheesy's coming over to get the

money you owe him, and oh yah… he's wants to kill you."

Now Leslie is scared. Caplinski puts his finger to his mouth in a signal for her to be quiet.

Caplinski: "We'll be in the bedroom."

Both men quickly go to the bedroom located at the other end of the room. Leslie goes to the couch were Klein and Caplinski were sitting.

She reaches down between the cushions and retrieves her Gen 17 Glock. She tucks it in the waistband of her designer jeans at the small of her back under her silk Vera Wang shirt. There's another more impatient knock. She goes to door and opens it.

A very large black man fills the entire doorway. Tiny pushes Leslie out of the way and walks in followed by Chessy in his black leather embossed cowboy hat and motorcycle jacket. Tiny takes his position between the couch and the chair closest to the front of the apartment, while Chessy takes a seat on couch. He looks down at the computer were *Dexter* is covering a room in plastic sheeting.

Cheesy: "Shit… I knew we forgot something. Tiny… next time remind me to bring some plastic sheeting. It makes things so much neater."
Tiny: "Sure boss, I'll make a note of it."
Cheesy: "While I talk to our detective friend here, why don't you look around and see if you can find all that money that doesn't belong to her."

Tiny starts searching the room by pulling up seat cushions,

knocking books and knick-knacks off the shelves, opening drawers and throwing their contents on the floor.
Tiny: "The room's clean, boss."

Leslie is standing by the window leaning back on the windowsill calculating how long it would take her to reach for her gun and drop Cheesy and his bodyguard. The emaciated Cheesy wasn't a problem, one bullet anywhere important would do the trick, but she'd need an elephant gun to take down Tiny.

Cheesy: "Check the bedroom."

Tiny walks to the back of the room and opens the bedroom door. Klein and Caplinski are standing there. Tiny goes in pushing the door closed behind him.

Klein whispers, "Make it loud."

The three men all start pulling things apart. Drawers are open, bras, underwear, cashmere sweaters, and designer shirts are scattering all over the room. The money is not there. The three men all look at one another. Tiny opens the door and goes back into the living room.

Tiny: "Nothing boss. She must have the dough hidden someplace else."
Cheesy: "Where's the money bitch?"
Leslie: "I spent it. You're not the only drug dealer in town."
Cheesy: "I'm not surprised. Well what are going to do? That's business, you win some and you lose some."

Cheesy gets up and rearranges his cowboy hat at a dapper

angle. He looks at Leslie but speaks to Tiny.

Cheesy: "Kill her." Chessy starts moving towards the door.
Tiny: "I'm not fucking killing anyone. You want her dead. Kill
her yourself."

Chessy stops, puts his hands on his hips, and thinks for a
second. He looks at Leslie.

Cheesy: "You see! I have to do everything myself. You just can't
get good help anymore."

Chessy pulls his piece from under his red and black leather
motorcycle jacket and haphazardly aims it at Tiny. He shoots
hitting Tiny in the shoulder. The big man hits the floor with a
loud groan.

Caplinski followed by Klein run into the living room guns
drawn. Cheesy sees Caplinski and fires hitting him in the arm
giving Leslie enough time to draw her weapon and shoot. She
drops Cheesy with one perfectly aimed shot to the forehead.
His gun skitters across the hardwood floor to Leslie's feet. She
drops her piece and picks up Cheesy's. She takes aim at Klein.
BANG! Leslie's body slams hard into the window her head
cracking the glass. BANG! BANG!

The next two shots hit her with the force of an elephant gun
putting her right through the cracked window. Tiny staggers to
his feet blood staining his tight black polo shirt. Klein helps
Caplinski to the couch.

Klein: "You guys all right?"
Caplinski: "Do I look all right? That asshole shot me!"

Tiny manages to get to one of the black leather chairs and deposits his oversized frame into the soft black leather. The impact of Tiny's body on the chair releases a final gasp of air from the deflated cushion.

Caplinski: "I got to check Leslie; she went out the window with the gun still in her hand."
Klein: "You two just stay where you are and call for re-enforcements. I'll check for the gun."

Klein runs downstairs as quickly as possible. When he gets to the street he sees what left of Leslie's body spread-eagled across her badly dented Austin Healy. Her body hit the sports car with such force that it popped the trunk open. The Doorman is bending over ready to pick up Cheesy's gun that landed on the sidewalk.

Klein: "Don't touch that! Go up to 408 and check on the two cops. They've been shot."

It's not exactly true but it will get the Doorman out of the way for a few minutes. He figures that all he needs. The Doorman stops what he's doing and goes into the building heading for the elevator.

Police and ambulance sirens can already be heard. They'd be on the scene any minute. Klein takes a cursory look at Leslie. She was dead before she went through the window. He goes around to the back of the Healey and looks in the trunk. He sees the brown paper bag filled with Cheesy's money and the missing leather attaché case that belongs to Donald Davis. He removes the paper bag and the attaché case and puts them in the trunk of his car.

People start coming out of the surrounding buildings to see what the commotion is all about. As they gather Klein positions himself beside Cheesy's gun making sure no numskull bystander tries to retrieve a souvenir. The police and ambulance arrive.

EPILOGUE

Mount Sinai Hospital, Tiny Wilson's Room

Tiny sits up in his hospital bed surrounded by flowers, balloons, and even a big Teddy Bear with a ribbon. Jake Klein sits in a chair beside him.

Klein: "So what do say?"
Tiny: "Private eyes? I don't know."
Klein: "It's better than working for a drug dealer, besides you're a hero. It's all over the papers. And Freddie said he'd farm out some of his business to us."
Tiny: "Who's got money to start a business?"
Klein: "I got that covered. With Cheesy's contribution and the money Davis promised me we got enough to get started."

A small lumpy package wrapped in newspaper and a red bow flies across the room and lands in Klein's lap. Caplinski appears in the doorway.

Caplinski: "I should have known you'd get your hands on the cash somehow."

Klein holds up the package. "Nice wrapping job. What is it?"
Caplinski: "Open it and see."

Klein removes the bow and carefully unwraps the lumpy package. It's his gold cricket money clip.

THE END

The Bastard

JERRY BADER

バスタード

PART I

BASUTADO

THE BASTARD

CARMAN

1987, Mount Sinai Hospital, Maternity Ward

A nurse wearing scrubs and a stethoscope walks quickly down the hospital hallway and enters the room of Kiku Kimura. The new mother is still groggy from the recent birth. The nurse takes a quick look at the chart at the foot of the bed to confirm she has the right patient. The nurse then moves to the side of the bed and checks the woman's IV. She adjusts the flow of the sedative drip. The baby is in a bassinet beside the mother's hospital bed. The nurse bends down to see the baby is sleeping.

Kiku: "What is it? Is something wrong?"

Nurse/Carman: "Not to worry sweetie, everything is fine. You have a healthy baby boy. I'm just taking him down for a few standard tests. You get some sleep now, and he'll be waiting for you when you wake up. He'll be hungry, so you better take a nap while you can."

The woman makes an effort to speak, but she reluctantly gives in to the increased amount of sedative. Kiku Kimura's eyes close. The nurse bundles the baby boy in an extra blanket and quickly heads down the hall and through the door marked "Stairs." A large man in a dark suit is waiting for her on the landing. Together the nurse and the man work their way down the steps to the basement-parking garage.

The man opens the basement garage door where a black funeral parlor limousine with dark-tinted windows is waiting.

The back door swings open. The nurse and the large man get in. Sitting in the back of the limousine is another heavy-set, rough looking man in a dark suit smoking a large cigar. The nurse still holding the baby takes the bench seat facing the back of the limo and the two men. The nurse taps twice on the Plexiglas panel that separates the Driver from the back of the limousine. The Driver in the front starts the engine and takes off for the exit.

Nurse/Carman: "Jesus Christ, put the fucking cigar out, there's a baby in the car."
Nikkie: "This ain't just a cigar boss, it's a *Cohiba Esplendido*, thirty-four bucks a pop."
Nurse: "I don't care if you're sucking on a diamond-studded dildo. Put the fucking thing out."

The second man grabs the cigar out of the cigar man's mouth and stubs it out in the ashtray.

Luka: "Don't be an asshole Nikkie. Do as you're told, the baby's worth more than your stinky cigar."
Nikkie: "*Ty che blyad? Suka blyad!* You owe me thirty-four bucks."

Luka gives Nikkie a look that says try to collect. Everyone remains quiet as the limo turns onto the turnpike.

KIKU

Mount Sinai Hospital, Maternity Ward

A young nurse enters the room of Kiku Kimura. She takes a look at the chart then moves to the side of the bed to check the seemingly sleeping new mother. She feels for a pulse on her wrist.

Nurse 2: "Son of a bitch!"

She tries to check the pulse in the mother's neck. Nothing. She presses the code button
.

Hospital Loud Speaker: "Paging Dr. Black, Room 893… Paging Dr. Black, Room 893… *Paging Dr. Black* is code for a patient in distress. Not something the hospital wants to broadcast to the rest of the mothers on the ward. There's the sudden sound of frantic activity in the hall. The nurse checks on the baby but the baby isn't there. She turns to the door just as a doctor and two nurses rush in wheeling a crash cart."

Nurse 2: "He's gone!"

The doctor rushes to the bedside and checks the woman's heart. He rips open Kiku's hospital gown and places the paddles on her Cherry Blossom tattooed chest.

Doctor: "Charge!"

The woman's body heaves up off the bed and lands with a thud.

Doctor: "Charge!"

He tries three times, each time KIMURA'S body is lifted off the bed, but each time the eerie flat digital sound of death continues to fill the room.

Doctor: "Again God damn it!"

No response... the doctor mumbles under his breath.

Doctor: "What the hell happened? She was fine a few hours ago." The DOCTOR sighs in frustration at his failure to save Kiku's life. He checks his watch.

Doctor: "Time of death 8:47 AM."
Nurse 2: "The baby's gone! He's not here!"
Doctor: "What are you talking about?"
Nurse 2: "The baby isn't in the bassinet. He's gone."

THE DRIVER

The home of Carman Antipov, the estranged wife of Russian mobster *Bol'shoy* Boris Antipov.

The Driver pulls up in front of a large house in the exclusive Bel-Air Estates. The two men in suits get out and wait for the nurse and the baby. The woman is obviously in charge. She taps on the window separating the Driver from the back of the limousine. The Driver slides back the Plexiglas panel so he can hear the woman's instructions.

Nurse/Carman: "You know what to do?"
Driver: "Yes Ma'am. Take the limo to Ralph's Salvage and make sure it's disposed of properly. There's a black Fiat Spider waiting for me. Bring it back to the house."
Nurse/Carman: "Good. When you get back, you'll be paid. And then I never want to see your handsome *punum* ever again."
Driver: "Yes, Ma'am."

The nurse gets out of the car with the sleeping baby and heads for the front of the house with the two thugs. The Driver starts the engine and heads out to Ralph's Salvage.

It takes a half hour for the Driver to get to Ralph's. The whole while he's thinking, *'what the hell have I got myself into?'* He's only a driver for hire. He answers a Want Ad in the Times for a one-day gig. That's all he knew. The whole thing seemed sketchy from the start, but how do you turn down twenty-five hundred dollars for one day's work. It was just too good to be legit, but he needed the money, and twenty-five hundred dollar paydays don't come around too often. He put the whole thing out of his mind. He did what he needed to do to survive, and that was that. Once it was over he'd be gone with twenty-five hundred bucks in his pocket, and hopefully, a fresh start.

The Driver enters the front gate of the salvage yard and pulls up in front of a ramshackle building that was badly in need of a paint job, and a few other repairs like a new roof, foundation, and walls.

A grizzled old man with a mop of messy white hair and tobacco-stained teeth comes out to greet him. He's wearing filthy jeans and a torn denim work shirt. The Driver stops the engine and gets out of the car.

Ralph: "Just leave her there; I'll get to it after lunch."
Driver: "I'm supposed to wait to make sure it gets done."
Ralph: "Jesus… everybody's in a fucking hurry these days. You young people got to learn to slow-the-fuck-down, or you'll have a heart attack."
Driver: "Those are my instructions. You want to speak to the lady."
Ralph: "Fuck No! I don't want to speak to the lady. She's worse than a heart attack."

Grumbling all the while, the old man gets into the limousine and drives it over to a waiting crane standing next to a giant compactor. The old man gets out of the limo and signals the crane operator. The Driver watches as the big black car is lifted into the oversized mechanical vise. In a matter of minutes the shiny black limousine that went missing from the August Brothers Funeral Home last night is nothing more than a large cube of scrap metal. The old man walks over to the Driver and hands him a set of keys.

Ralph: "Your ride is parked behind the office. If I was you I'd be careful. That's the Tsarina's car, and she's kind of particular."

The Driver nods and heads to the back of the building that the old man euphemistically called his office. The car is nice: a metallic black exterior with beige leather seats, black piping, and a real wood panel dashboard. He gets in the Spider and heads back to the house.

SATO

Mount Sinai Hospital, Maternity Ward

A youthful looking, expensively dressed, forty-five-year-old Japanese woman carrying her pretty eighteen-month-old granddaughter walks briskly down the corridor followed by two hard-looking Japanese tough-guys. The woman is dressed fashionably in an oriental-inspired high-collared dress with a slit up the side.

Her clothes fit in a manner that emphasizes a still youthful body while discreetly covering the elaborate *tebori irezumi* style *Jigoku Dayua* tattoo that wraps around her torso.
The men are wearing black suits, white shirts, and black ties with red Cherry Blossom stickpins.

Sato Kimura Muonna is Kiku's mother and the grandmother to Kato, Kiku's now orphaned daughter. Sato is not your typical *obaasan* or Japanese grandmother, not unless you call a Yakuza nightclub owner who also runs a stable of high-end prostitutes typical. She is the widow of a murdered Yakuza *Oyabun*, Ito Muonna, who ran the nightclub and prostitution ring with Sato as his *Chi-san*, club manager.

The idea of an *Onna-Oyabun* or female Yakuza boss is often thought of as a myth created for the movies. They are rare, but they do exist; and if you ever run into one, stay clear because they are a special kind of trouble. Surviving in a male-dominated environment that treats women like property requires a unique combination of female charm, physical toughness, and mental discipline. In simple terms... you don't fuck with *Onna-Oyabun* Muonna.

Kiku's Doctor is standing behind the nurses' station checking some paper work. He sees Sato and her two bodyguards coming down the corridor so he goes around the counter to greet her.

Doctor: "Mrs. Muonna…"

Sato reaches the nurses' station, hands Kato to one of her bodyguards, and starts in on the Doctor.

Sato: "What the hell kind of hospital is this? My daughter comes in here to have a baby, and you fucking kill her?"
Doctor: "Now just a minute Mrs. Muonna…"

The bodyguard holding Kato puts the child down. Both men take an ominous step forward towards the Doctor. The Doctor stumbles awkwardly backwards banging into the counter of the nurses' station knocking some flowers into the lap of the nurse sitting behind it.

Sato: "You haven't heard the last of this young man. You and your death trap institution will be hearing from my lawyers."

Kato moves beside the Doctor's leg. She tugs on his white hospital lab coat. He looks down at the little girl and smiles. She hits him in the knee.

Sato: "Now… where the hell is my grandson?"

WHAT A MESS!

The home of Carman Antipov.

The Driver makes it back to the house faster than he'd expected. Driving the Spider was a gas, and it was sure a hell of a lot more fun to drive than a big old clunky stolen funeral parlor limousine. He parks the car in the driveway and makes his way to the back of the house as instructed when he was hired. The large glass sliding door to the patio is partly open; he assumes, left open for him. He enters the house.

The patio door leads to an eating area off to the side of the kitchen. No one seems to be around, and all he can hear is the muffled sounds of the baby whimpering. He makes his way through the house lead by the baby's cry. He gets to the living room and stops.

The two men from the limo are lying on their backs; pools of blood act as liquid pillows, no doubt from the matching holes in their foreheads. Two Colt Defender handguns lie on the thick pile Persian carpet, one beside each man.

A stout older gentlemen with stylishly cut gray hair and an expensive bespoke charcoal pinstriped suit ruined by the hole in his chest sits opposite the entrance to the room. Behind him is a large marble fireplace. Above the fireplace is an oversized portrait of an elegantly dressed woman that looks like the nurse. A Walther PPQ M2 handgun hangs limply from his right hand. The old man must have caught the two thugs as they entered the room before they could react.

The nurse is lying face down at the other end of the room. Pieces of her skull float on top of an ever-expanding stain that surrounds what's left of her head. She clearly tried to make a run for it but didn't quite make it. It looks like an ambush gone wrong. The Nurse is holding a Colt Defender in her right hand and the baby cradled in her left arm.

She obviously got off the shot that killed the fat guy in the chair, but unfortunately for her, it didn't do the job fast enough. The old man must have got her trying to escape. She attempted to protect the child as she fell but was probably dead before she hit the ground. The scene was a mess.

The Driver picks up the crying baby and tries to settle it down. It must be hungry. He couldn't just leave it there. He couldn't call the cops. He was party to something very wrong, but he didn't know what. His options were limited. He had to get out of there fast but what the hell was he going to do with the kid? Maybe he could drop it off at the hospital? No that was too dangerous. He could leave it at a church or synagogue? No… he wouldn't do that either.

He goes through the ground floor of the house and finds a laundry room with a plastic basket filled with neatly folded bath towels. He creates a little bed in the basket from the towels and puts the baby in the middle.

He finds a knapsack in the kitchen filled with diapers, formula, and supplies designed for a newborn. He slings the knapsack over his shoulder, picks up the basket, and heads out the patio doors. He puts the baby on the floor on the passenger side of the Spider and the knapsack on the seat. He starts the engine and takes off, never to be seen or heard from again.

The next morning the papers are full of the news:

RUSSIAN BRATVA BOSS BUTCHERED

Gazette Staff Reporter… Russian Mobster Bol'shoy Boris Antipov, his estranged wife, Carman, and two of her bodyguards were found dead last night in her luxury Bel-Air Estates home. The Antipov's two-year-old daughter, Carla, was found safe, asleep in an upstairs bedroom.

Carla Antipov stands to inherit her father's substantial business empire. Antipov's close friend, lawyer, and business associate, Malcolm Sokolov, released a statement this morning stating he would act as Carla's guardian until she comes of age.

MOBSTER'S MISTRESS CROAKS, BABY DISAPPEARS

In a related story Antipov's long-time mistress, Kiku Kimura, died due to an overdose of painkillers after giving birth to Antipov's only son who mysteriously disappeared from the hospital yesterday. A police spokeswoman said the Coroner has ruled Kimura's death an accidental overdose. They have no leads on Kimura's missing baby

.

Kiku Kimura is survived by a daughter Kato, her mother Sato Muonna, and the missing baby boy. Sato announced that she has guardianship of the little girl and will use whatever resources she has available to try and find her missing grandson.

PART II

Goi

THE AGREEMENT

MALCOLM

Present Day.
Parking garage of the Tanoshii Basho Shopping Mall

A vintage dark maroon Bentley S2 Continental Coupé pulls into the parking garage of the Tanoshii Basho Shopping Mall. In the back is seventy-eight year-old Malcolm Sokolov, Chairman of The Bolshoy Land Development Company.

The valet parking attendant is familiar with the Bentley and raises the barricade to let it pass through. The driver, Ransom Konnors, stops the Bentley in front of the attendant and rolls down the window

Attendant: "You can go right in. He's down on the *Gozu* Level in the usual spot. We've closed the level so no other cars are on it."

Each parking level is marked with a legendary Japanese creature supposedly making it easier for people to remember where they parked. More likely it's a subtle jab played on the well-heeled Caucasian shoppers who have no idea what these creatures represent. *Gozu,* or Ox-Face, is a creature with a man's body and an ox's face, that along with his partner *Mezu,* or Horse-Face, guard the underworld, an appropriate symbol for the meeting that was about to take place.

Attendant: "People are pissed, especially the women. God forbid there's no valet parking and they have to walk up the stairs."
Ransom hands the Attendant an envelope.

Ransom: "That should cover the inconvenience... what about the cameras?"
Attendant: "All looked after... technical problems all morning. You know how it is with high-tech stuff."
Ransom: "Good. We were never here. Understand?"
Attendant: "Yes sir, understood!"

Ransom rolls up the window and proceeds to The *Gozu* Level. In the corner in the back is a black Cadillac limousine. Ransom pulls the Bentley in beside the Cadillac so the back passenger seat of the Bentley is only inches away from the back driver's side seat of the Caddie. The back windows of both cars roll down.

Malcolm: "Mr. Mayor..."
Mayor: "Malcolm..."
Malcolm: "Everything is arranged. My people will make the first payment tomorrow. The package will be waiting in locker 893. The key will be mailed to the post office box you gave me. It's all arranged. You just make sure that bylaw doesn't get passed."
Mayor: "Listen, that bitch Muonna is working hard to see it gets through Council."
Malcolm: "That's why you're getting paid... to make sure that doesn't happen. You really don't want to disappoint us Charlie, you really don't!"
Mayor: "It won't pass. Just make sure I get the key before the vote next week. I don't get the key, there's nothing I can do."
Malcolm: "You'll get it."

The window of the Mayor's car rolls up abruptly ending the conversation.

Malcolm: "Asshole! Okay Ransom, Take me back to the office."
Ransom: "Yes sir…"

The Cadillac waits until the Bentley pulls out and leaves the parking garage. Once Malcolm's car has safely left, the Mayor tells his driver to take him back to city hall. As the Caddie approaches the exit, the chauffeur sees it's blocked by a large wooden sawhorse with a sign reading "NO EXIT."

Mayor: "What's going on? Why are you stopping?"

Behind the sawhorse is an older but still trim well-dressed Sato Muonna with two large humorless Japanese bodyguards standing behind her. One of the bodyguards is holding a large brown envelope.

Mayor: "Fuck! Where the hell did she come from?"

JUST A DRIVER

Back office at The Bolshoy Land Development Company

Ransom Konnors sits at his desk drawing on a five-by-seven sketchpad. He's a handsome man with vaguely Japanese features that seem to have been carefully selected out of a mixed bag of desirable traits.

He always wanted to be an artist; to create, to make something out of nothing, but instead he was a driver like his father. Don't misunderstand, he loved his father, and he respected what he did. But still, a driver was really nothing more than a glorified deliveryman; it was a job that neither paid enough money nor allowed enough time for him to acquire the skills needed to actually make his dream come true.

So Ransom's artistic aspirations faded to random doodling: more a therapeutic exercise in relaxation, than an actual creative process. If a life of creativity was not within reach, he would have to settle for his other motivating drive, to get what he was owed. A very attractive, stylishly dressed Japanese woman stands in the doorway.

Kate: "Hay Rembrandt put your crayons away. It's time. You don't want to keep Carla waiting."

Kate Kimura is an in-house lawyer at The Bolshoy, a land development firm with side interests in influence peddling, coercion, and political corruption. Kimura being a common Japanese name didn't setoff any alarm bells with either Carla or Malcolm who long since reduced the tragic death of Carla's father to ancient history. The fact that Kate was rumored to be

Carla's lover helped discourage any busybody that thought some research into Kate's past might be appropriate.

When speaking with her mother Kate never called Carla by name but instead referred to her as the *Futakuchhi-onna*: the legendary two-mouthed wife with an insatiable appetite.

The nominal boss of The Bolshoy was Carla Antipov, a strikingly, sophisticated woman raised by her father's long-time lawyer and confident, Malcolm Sokolov. Malcolm was the real boss who maintained control of all major decisions while Carla acted as the attractive face of the evil empire.

Their relationship was complicated. Sokolov was the only father she ever had. All she knew of her biological father was what Sokolov told her, that, a few old photographs, and some ancient newspaper stories found on the Internet.

Carla both loved and hated Sokolov. She relied on his experience but hated the fact he was the one in charge. Her real father built the company, and she was his only heir. The Bolshoy was her birthright, and Sokolov was nothing more than a hired hand.

Kate: "I'm waiting handsome."

Ransom closes his sketchpad, puts it in the desk drawer, and locks it. Kate and Ransom head down the corridor to the reception area and up a winding glass and metal staircase to the executive offices.

Antipov's secretary sees Kate and Ransom coming up the stairs. She picks up the phone and buzzes her boss.

Secretary: "Miss. Antipov… they're here."

She waits till they approach.

Secretary: "You can go right in."

Antipov's office is an elegant collection of classic Bauhaus design, all black leather and shiny chrome: all hard and cold like its occupant. There's no clutter, no papers scattered haphazardly on the black leather desk pad that covers the glass topped piece of sculpture that acts as her desk; no files piled up in an effort to show how hard she works; just a sterile demand for order, power, and respect. This is the office of a joyless hard ass.

The only color in the room is found in the two large de Kooning canvases that dominate the sidewalls: a reflection perhaps of the tortured soul that lay buried somewhere underneath a finely sculpted body that must have taken years on a treadmill to produce.

The boss lady herself stands looking out the expansive glass floor-to-ceiling window that overlooks the city. She may not be a warm and cuddly woman, but she is beautiful in her charcoal gray Valentino business suit. She turns to face Kate, ignoring Ransom.

Antipov: "The package is between the Wassilys."

She waves a dismissive hand at the two Marcel Breuer Wassily Chairs that stand guard in front of her glass and chrome desk. They're the kind of chairs that say, *'I'm rich, I'm sophisticated, and I want you out of my sight as soon as possible.'* Between the two chairs is a white plastic shopping bag with the words *The Baruku* printed on the side underneath some Japanese letters.

Antipov: "He'll take you to Little Tokyo, the Tanoshii Basho Mall, as we discussed last night."

She turns to face Ransom.

Antipov: "You enter the mall separately. Do not go in together. You're strangers, totally unrelated. You go to the bulk food store and buy something, any shit, as long as it's about the same size as the package. And make sure it's in the same kind of shopping bag."

Ransom thinks: *'these are not the instructions Malcolm gave me earlier.'*

Antipov: "Kate will put her package on the floor so she can pay for the locker. You do exactly the same thing at the same time. You put your package down right beside Kate's and pay for your locker." She looks at KATE.

Antipov: "You know what to do?"

Kate nods, but Antipov continues anyway. "You drop the key. Let him pick it up. You make a big fuss about how clumsy you are, distracting anyone watching while you pick up his package and place it in your locker."

Ransom: "Wait a second. Malcolm didn't say anything about this. He just said drop Kate off at the mall and circle the block till she comes out."

Antipov: "Things have changed. Just do what you're told, or do I have to find another driver?"

Ransom: "No Ma'am"

She looks back at Kate. "On the way out you put the key in the envelope Malcolm gave you and drop it in the mailbox." She turns back to Ransom.
Antipov: "You can't be seen together before the actual drop, and you can't be seen together after. Do you understand? Or do I have to go over this again?"
Ransom: "No Ma'am, I got it."
Antipov: "Stop fucking calling me Ma'am."
Kate: "Don't worry Carla. It's a straightforward exchange. Nothing will go wrong."
Antipov takes an menacing step closer to Ransom. "When it's done you come directly back here and bring me the second key. If Malcolm stops you and asks about the drop, you don't mention the switch. Now get out of here and get it done. And if you know what's good for you, nothing better happen to Kate. I hold you responsible."
Ransom: "Yes Ma'am, nothing will go wrong."

WHAT CAN GO WRONG?

First Street on the way to the Tanoshii Basho Mall

The drive to the Tanoshii Basho Mall seems uneventful. Kate sits nervously tapping her perfectly manicured fingernails on the elbow rest of Ransom's vintage Fiat Spider. Her other hand tightly grips the package for fear it might try to escape.

Neither Ransom nor Kate speak, both are intent on following Antipov's instructions to the letter. Ransom periodically checks the rear-view mirror to see if they are being followed. It's not that he expects anything, it's just a habit his father drilled into him, his words permanently etched into his subconscious.

Father's Voice: *"You always check. Never assume. Never take anything for granted. Most of the time nothing goes wrong, so you get lazy, you relax... BAM! You're fucked! You got to understand, sooner or later someone is going to try to screw you, so be prepared. Always check!"*

Ransom notices a Lincoln Navigator several car lengths back that seems to be shadowing his every move. Ransom pulls out and passes several cars before cutting back into line. Kate gives him a look of concern.

The Lincoln follows but almost clips a cab as it tries to tuck in behind a Honda Accord. The cabbie leans heavily on his horn. Kate starts to turn...

Ransom: "Don't look! Keep your eyes on the road ahead."
Kate: "What? Is something wrong? What's going on?"

Ransom thinks, why is she involved in this? This is just the kind of sketchy business his father warned him about. He expected it. He knew who his bosses were, and what they were capable of doing, but Kate was a real estate lawyer, not a bagman comfortable making illegal payoffs.

Ransom bided his time. He knew an alley ran from First Street all the way down to Central Avenue and the back entrance to the parking garage adjacent to the mall.

Ransom waits till the last moment; he pulls into the curb lane just as he approaches the alley. He turns the wheel hard right into the narrow back street used for truck deliveries. He watches in the rear mirror as the Navigator speeds past, unable to follow.

Ransom drives into the parking garage, collects the ticket stub from the automated machine, and proceeds down to the *Mezu*, Horse-Head Level. He finds a spot with a perfect view of any cars entering or leaving the level. He backs in so he's facing forward.

Ransom: "Just wait a minute. I want to see if the Lincoln was able to follow us."

They sit. Kate nervously taps her fingers while Ransom scans for trouble. He can hear her breathing hard as if she just ran a marathon in her expensive designer heels. He looks over. Her chest moves up and down in rhythmic syncopation with her tapping. She looks back at him.

Kate: "What do you expect? I'm nervous. You drive like a crazy person." Ransom doesn't respond.

Kate: "And stop looking at my tits. We have a job to do."
Ransom keeps it professional. Someone has too.

Ransom: "Relax… we lost them. You leave first. Use the stairs. I'll hang back but don't worry, I'll be right behind you."

Kate opens the door and stumbles slightly as she gets out of the car dropping the package.

Ransom: "Just hold it together a little longer. It will be over soon."

She gives him a dirty look, more embarrassed than nasty.

Kate: "I'm fine. You just do your part."

Ransom waits till she gets to the door marked *Mezu Horse-Head Stairs*, then he follows. As they go up the stairs, he watches the slightly built attractive lawyer struggle with the package but he remains well back. Every so often she turns to look to see if he's there. Her eyes meet his… she's out of her depth. She knows he knows and it makes her even more nervous.

Kate works her way up to Central Avenue and heads for the back entrance of the Tanoshii Basho Mall. The sidewalk is busy with pedestrians: a young Japanese man and woman holding hands walk a few feet behind Kate; a group of teenage girls all wearing private school blazers and too-short pleated skirts laugh and jostle as they snap selfies with each other. A short stocky Japanese businessman rushes past Ransom as if in a hurry to catch up to Kate.

Ransom picks up his pace passing the schoolgirls, more interested in keeping his partner safe than protecting the package. The man passes Kate without even a glance. Ransom relaxes a bit, but not much. He must stay alert.

The entire group moves through the doors of the mall together then scatters. Kate seems exhausted from carrying the package in those stupid high heels. She stops to sit on a bench in front of a Japanese Zen garden. She slips off her right heel and rubs her toes, hoping the brief respite will help the swelling go down. The next time she has to commit a felony she'll know to wear more comfortable shoes.

Ransom still has to put together the second package. He spots the boutique food store Antipov mentioned, *The Baruku.* It seems to specialize in all kinds of bulk food.

Antipov didn't even offer to pay for the stuff Ransom needed to buy… cheap bitch. He sees a display of birdseed in bags that look about the right size and weight. He picks up a bag and heads for the cashier. He notices a display of Eatmore Peanut Chews and realizes he's hungry.

He grabs one of the candy bars and places it and the birdseed in front of the young Japanese woman manning the cash register. She's preoccupied talking to a fellow cashier. She puts the birdseed and the Peanut Chew in a clear plastic bag.

Ransom: "Don't you have any *Baruku* bags?"
Cashier: "Really? You need a *Baruku* bag for your birdseed?
Ransom: "Yah… actually I do."

Exasperated, the cashier searches under the counter for a *Baruku* bag. She finally finds one and hands it to Ransom.

Cashier: "Happy?" The bag is black with a white *Baruku* logo underneath red Japanese letters.
Ransom: "It's black!"
Cashier: "Yah, it's black. "
Ransom: "Don't you have the white ones?"
Cashier: "What are you some kind of bigot?"
Ransom: "I need the white bag!"
Cashier: "The white bags are the old ones. We don't have them any more. The black ones are new. I really don't think your birds will care."

She forgets to charge him for the candy bar, but he gives her the money for it, anyway. She doesn't notice. She's more interested in telling her colleague what a shit her boyfriend is.

Ransom takes the Peanut Chew out of the bag, unwraps it, and takes a bite.

Ransom: "Damn... that's a good candy bar!"

Ransom looks around to see if he can spot any trouble. The mall is busy with shoppers, tourists, and school kids just getting out of class. An attendant at the Service Desk continually texts with one hand while handing out brochures to tourists with the other: a mark of singular dexterity, not manners.

He looks for Kate at the lockers, but she's not there. The teenage schoolgirls he saw earlier run past him giggling and laughing. One of the girls slams right into him dropping her phone on the terrazzo floor. She bends down to pick it up not bothering to apologize. She gives him a dirty look like it's his fault she dropped the damn thing. She runs off to catch up to her friends.

Kate is still resting on the bench waiting. She looks in his direction and spots the black plastic bag. She is not pleased. He's not sure if her displeasure is because of the bag or the candy bar he's eating. It dawns on him; he should have bought one for her.

He notices the stocky Japanese guy in the business suit looking in his direction. It's the same guy that passed him outside on his way into the mall. If he didn't know better, he could have sworn he saw a red Koi tattoo sneak out from under the cuff of his suit jacket. Not the kind of thing you usually see on a business executive, not unless his business was with the Yakuza.

Ransom checks the locker area and notices the couple that were holding hands are just standing around looking in Kate's direction.

Kate is about to stand, but he casually signals her to sit. She looks puzzled but catches on to his meaning. She sits back down and starts fumbling in her purse as if looking for something. The businessman starts moving towards Kate from one side and the romantic couple from the other.

Ransom walks quickly to where Kate is sitting as if he's late for a rendezvous with his wife. She stands not sure what's happening. When he reaches her, he grabs her package so that he has both bags in one hand.

With the other hand he hugs her, bringing her close so he can kiss her on the cheek. She's startled by his action but plays along. She's nervous, but she's smart. She knows something has gone wrong. He takes her arm with his free hand and leads her to the *Kabuteru Lounge* at the far side of the mall.

Kate: "What the hell are you doing?" They continue to walk. Ransom: "We're surrounded. The big guy in the business suit and the couple holding hands have been tailing you ever since you left the parking garage."

Kate starts to look around. She catches sight of the three people in question all headed in the same direction. They get to the lounge and grab a table. The businessman waits outside the bar on a bench facing the lounge entrance. The romantic couple enters the bar and takes a table at the opposite side of the room.

Ransom: "Order us a drink. I'll be back in a few minutes."
Kate: "You gotta go now? Can't you hold it for Christ's sake?"
Ransom" "Just order the damn drinks." He gets up to leave taking both packages.
Kate: "Wait!" Ransom stops.
Ransom: "What?"
Kate: "What do you want to drink?" Ransom looks at her like she's crazy.
Ransom: "Order me a Trojan Horse."
Kate: "A what?"
He leans over the table and kisses her on the cheek again.

Ransom: "Order any fucking thing you want."

He heads to the men's room. He finds a stall and enters. He opens the white *Baruku* bag. It contains a large parcel wrapped in brown paper. He assumes it's cash, a lot of cash, whatever it is, it's valuable, and a lot of people seem interested in getting their hands on it.

He opens the black *Baruku* bag and exchanges the birdseed for the package and the package for the birdseed.

He flushes the toilet, grabs both packages and opens the stall door. Standing directly in front of him is the Yakuza businessman with the Koi tattoo. He's holding a Remington R51 Crimson Trace handgun aimed directly at Ransom 's chest.

Businessman: "Hand over the white bag."

As Ransom was about to hand the guy the bag, someone else leaves a neighboring stall.

Bathroom Guy: "What the hell's going on here?"

The businessman swings his arm around catching the poor fellow in the face with the side of his Remington, as he does, Ransom kicks the Businessman in the groin doubling him over in agony. The civilian is on the floor bleeding all over the white tile. The Businessman is on his knees groaning in pain.

Ransom goes directly to where Kate is sitting. She has already downed what looks like a highball of something strong with another sitting waiting for him. Ransom gets to the table and pulls Kate out of her chair.

Kate: "What's going on?"

Ransom: "Here… take the package and put it in the locker."

He hands her the white *Baruku* bag. There's a lot of noise and commotion coming from the area around the men's room. Several people from the bar go to see what's going on. Kate looks at Ransom.

Kate: "What the hell did you do?"
Ransom: "Just put the bag in the locker."

She takes the package from Ransom and with her free hand grabs Ransom's drink and downs it in one gulp. They both head for the lockers. The romantic couple spot Kate and Ransom moving towards the lockers. They get up and follow. Kate gets to Locker 893 opens it and places the package inside. She puts the money in the slot and shuts the door. The package is safe. She breathes a sigh of relief. Meanwhile Ransom has locked the black bag in his locker.

Kate thinks: '*this isn't the right scenario, everything is messed up.*' She remembers she's supposed to drop the key. Not sure it even matters anymore she drops it anyway. It clinks as it hits the terrazzo floor. Ransom goes to pick it up but stops. He feels the pressure of a handgun jammed up against his kidneys held by the male partner of the romantic couple. His female colleague steps between Kate and Ransom and picks up the key.

Romantic Woman: "Now you two just relax and have a seat on that nice wooden bench while we quietly leave. Do not think about following us. It would be a mistake, your last mistake."

The romantic couple watch as Kate and Ransom go to the bench and sit. The two lovers walk hand-in-hand towards the exit like they're just another husband and wife out for a good time on date night.

THE AFTERMATH

The Office of Carla Antipov,
The Bolshoy Land Development Company

Carla sits behind her glass and chrome desk. She appears surprisingly calm considering everything that can go wrong did go wrong. Malcolm sits in one of the Wassily Chairs; lines of anger punctuate the craggy details etched into his well-worn face. Kate Kimura sits legs crossed in the other chair still a bit unnerved by the day's events. Ransom stands off to the side as if an afterthought; after all, he's just the driver.

Malcolm: "Does somebody want to tell me what the hell happened? All you had to do was put the package in the locker and mail the goddamn key. How fucking hard can that be?"

Kate turns to answer but Malcolm isn't finished. He looks up at Ransom. "And you… I told you to stay in the car and circle the block till Kate came out. Goddamn it! Doesn't anybody follow instructions anymore?"
Ransom: "We were tailed."
Malcolm: "What do you mean you were tailed?"
Ransom: "Somebody knew about the drop. Whoever it was has plenty of resources. They had a whole crew following us, either that, or there were multiple teams involved."
Malcolm: "Goddamn Sato. It must have been her. She'll do anything to see that bylaw gets passed."
Carla: "Take it easy Malcolm… I'll meet with the Mayor after the fundraiser tonight and see if I can make another arrangement."

Malcolm gets up from the chair.

Malcolm: "Listen Carla, I hate that you have to be with that clown, but if he gets to be Governor, this Tanoshii Basho business will be small potatoes."
Carla: "I know Malcolm. I know… you leave the Mayor to me. After tonight he'll do anything I ask."

Malcolm leaves the room shaking his head in frustration still mumbling something about incompetence and ineptitude. When he's safely out of earshot Ransom turns to Carla.

Ransom: "Miss Antipov, do you want the other key."
Carla: "Now what would I want with a goddamn bag of birdseed?"
Ransom: "Well it's not exactly…"
Carla: "Do you mind? Go back to your office and wait till you're needed. In fact I got a better idea, go back to the mall and stake out the locker and see who picks up the package."
Ransom: "But…"
Carla: "Didn't you hear me? Get over to the mall before the damn thing disappears."
Ransom: "Yes Ma'am."
Carla: "Didn't I tell you not to call me Ma'am?"
Ransom: "Yes Ma'am."
Carla: "Get the hell out of here."

THE PICKUP

Tanoshii Basho Shopping Mall

Ransom sits on the bench next to the Japanese rock garden munching on another Peanut Chew while keeping an eye on the lockers. It's raining outside and he's still a little damp from the walk from the parking garage to the mall entrance.

He notices a young woman and her two small children make their way to the locker area. It looks like the woman is heading directly to Locker 893. He stands, finishes the last bite of the candy bar and throws the wrapper in the recycle bin. He sidesteps a few shoppers making his way across the mall to where the woman is standing.

She puts the key in the locker and opens it. Ransom stops. There's no package, just three yellow rain slickers, two little ones for the kids, and one adult-sized one for the mother.

Ransom: "Excuse me Ma'am, but do you still need the locker?" The Woman: "Help yourself young man we're leaving." The kids start to argue whether Mario is more powerful than Luigi. The Woman: "Now you two behave yourselves. We're going home, and if you're good, Mommy will buy you PEZ."

The last time Ransom heard anybody mention PEZ was when he was ten years old. Maybe the next time he'd get some PEZ instead of a Peanut Chew. The woman takes one kid in each hand and heads for the exit. The package is gone. Ransom opens his locker with the key Carla didn't want. The black plastic *Baruku* bag is still there. He takes the bag and leaves the mall.

CARLA AND THE MAYOR

The Pink Palace Hotel, The Garden Bungalow Suite.

The Mayor is sitting on the edge of the king-sized canopy bed putting on his shoes. The bed looks as if it has seen a considerable amount of activity. Carla steps out of the shower and wraps herself in a towel. The Mayor puts on his suit jacket. Carla goes to him. She straightens his tie and kisses him.

Carla: "Are you sure you have to go right now?"
Mayor: "My wife is up in the suite and she'll be wondering what happened to me."
Carla: "She saw how you were mobbed after the speech. She'll just figure you're meeting with a reporter or one of your aids."
Mayor: "You know I want to stay, but at this stage of the game we have to be careful. No mistakes, no slip-ups. There are reporters dogging me around every corner. It wasn't easy sneaking out to the bungalow."
Carla: "Okay, if you insist, but you don't know what you're missing. Anyway, I wouldn't use that expression anymore.
Mayor: "What expression is that?"
Carla: "*Dogging* is Internet slang for people having sex in public. Not a turn of phrase the next Governor should be using."
Mayor: "Really? Jesus, doesn't anybody speak English anymore?" She lets the towel drop to the floor.
Carla: "Speaking of sex..."
Mayor: "I assure you sweetheart, I know exactly what I'm missing." He takes on a more serious tone.
Mayor: "And speaking of what I'm missing... there's the matter of a missing key."

Carla moves to a chair where her clothes are haphazardly strewn. She starts to dress.

Carla: "I told you Malcolm is a fool. He can't do anything right. You get that bylaw passed then I can oust him from the company. Once I've got full control, I can funnel you whatever you need. When you're Governor we'll be unstoppable."
Mayor: "In the meantime I could use the money. You tell Malcolm I don't get the package, the bylaw goes through."
Carla: "I'll tell him; but that bylaw has to go through no matter what."
Mayor: "Yah, well we don't have to tell him that, do we? Anyway I got to go before I'm missed."

He looks in the full-length mirror and smiles a practiced politician's smile.

Mayor: "Now that's what a Governor should look like."

He leaves. After the door closes Carla finds her cell phone and calls Kate.

Carla: "Kate, where are you?"

Kate is naked in bed in Carla's penthouse condominium. Carla's bedroom like her office is a cold, monotone environment except for the splash of color provided by the large abstract expressionist canvas that hangs behind the black lacquer platform bed.

Kate: "I'm in bed waiting for you."
Carla: "Good, I'm on my way there now."
Kate: "I hope he didn't tire you out too much…"

Carla: "You just be awake when I get home."
Kate: "Did you get the video?"

Kate goes over to the desk at the side of the room to fetch her brief case. She opens the case revealing a custom interior that is actually set up with a small digital camera. She flips open the view screen and presses a button. It's a crystal clear image of the Mayor on top of her. His face is clearly visible while her's is hidden by some strategically positioned bed sheets.

Carla: "I got it."

PART III

SHO

The Prize

SATO AND RANSOM

The apartment of Ransom Konnors

It's been a long day and Ransom is tired. He looks forward to a quiet evening doing absolutely nothing. He walks up to his apartment on the third floor of a remodeled triplex.

The apartment is big for the rent he pays and for the neighborhood he lives in, but his landlord, the sweet elderly Mrs. Shinigami likes him. If she needs anything done around the building, he's always more than willing to help. Besides... any time she sees him she teaches him a new Japanese word, something that might come in handy one day.

He's still holding the black *Baruku* bag as he turns the key to his apartment. As he enters, he notices the lights are on. He hears the sound of people talking in the living room. As he approaches the entrance, he sees the ancient Mrs. Shinigami serving tea to Kate and an older Japanese woman; the woman looks like what Kaye might look like in her seventies.

His apartment is not only big it is stylishly decorated in an eclectic mix of Japanese art, rosewood tables, and soft as butter black leather couches, all in perfect Parson's style proportions. Some people spend their money on partying, Ransom spends it on furniture and art, things that go beyond the ephemeral pleasures.

Mrs. Shinigami holds up a cup of tea and gestures for him to take a seat on the black leather couch across from the two rosewood Forbannelse chairs occupied by Kate and the other woman.

Mrs. Shinigami: "I hope you don't mind my dear? After all…
you're all family."

Ransom sits and accepts the cup of tea. He places the black
Baruku bag on the floor beside his foot. Mrs. Shinigami bows to
each of them and leaves.

Sato: "Mrs. Shinigami is an old family friend. She was kind
enough to let us in while we waited. Our late husbands were
business partners."

Ransom turns to Kate

Ransom: "Do you mind telling me what's going on here?"
Kate: "I think our grandmother should explain."
Ransom: "Our grandmother?"

Sato starts to tell him the story of his birth, about his real
mother and father, and how the man Ransom knows as his
father rescued him from the carnage following the kidnapping.

She explains that Carla's mother was determined to protect her
daughter's inheritance knowing that Boris would eventually
opt to give his only son control of the family business.

Carman's plan was to kidnap the baby and have him put up for
adoption as an abandoned child. Boris got wind of the plan, but
his attempted rescue ended in a blood bath.

Sato: "You are my grandson, and Kato, not Kate, is your half
sister. I tracked down your surrogate Father, the Driver, and
we privately kept in touch while you were growing up. It is not

an accident that you got a job working at The Bolshoy, or that you live here. Now it's time for you and your sister to take what rightfully belongs to you."

Ransom is looking directly at Sato. He turns to look at Kate.

Ransom: "Did you know about this?"

Kate nods.

Ransom: "And exactly how are a grandmother, a real estate lawyer, and a chauffeur going to take control of a mob-controlled company?"

Sato: "To start you can give me that *Baruku* bag and then I'll explain exactly who I am, what I do, and who our friends are."

THE PINK SLIP

The office of Carla Antipov

Carla sits at her desk nervously waiting for a call from a staffer who's attending the City Council vote on the bylaw to allow the redevelopment of the Tanoshii Basho Mall. The phone rings.

Carla: "Carla Antipov… yes… yes… that's wonderful, thank you. No, you don't have to come back. Take the rest of the afternoon off. Sure, that's fine, all right, have one for me."

Carla hangs up, smiles, and gets up from her glass and chrome desk. She heads across the executive lobby to Malcolm's office. She stands just inside his office entrance. Malcolm sits dejected behind his big solid walnut antique desk.

Carla: "You heard?"

Malcolm nods.

Malcolm: "I knew I couldn't trust that goddamn politician."
Carla: "Listen Malcolm I think it's time for you to go. This scheme of yours just didn't work out. I appreciate everything you've done for me over the years but this is my company, and I intend to run it my way. It needs new blood. Why not retire gracefully? We'll throw a big shindig; even give you a gold watch with your name engraved on the back."
Malcolm: *Yebat Suka!* Retire… really, you want me to retire? Listen to me you snarky tight-ass bitch! I'm not going anywhere. This is just a minor setback. Shit happens. I helped build this company with your father, and the only fucking way I'm leaving is horizontally in a box.

Carla remains calm.

Carla: "All right Malcolm, if that's the way you want it, horizontally in a box it will be."

Carla turns and starts to leave his office, already planning her next move.

Malcolm: "*Suka*! Retire my ass… Who does she think she is?"

Carla doesn't respond or look back as she crosses the lobby to her office. Malcolm takes the cell phone from his jacket pocket and selects a number.

Malcolm: "It's me… send me something special tonight, understand, something very special. I'm in that kind of mood."

Once Carla gets back to her office, she picks up the phone on her desk and speaks to her secretary.

Carla: "Tell that driver to come see me. And let me know the next time Malcolm needs to use him."

COLLATERAL DAMAGE

The *Shizukana Basho* Private Club

Sato, Kate, Ransom, and an elderly Japanese man sit around a low-to-the-floor dark stained bamboo table. The table is surrounded by four chairs with wide flat bamboo bars forming the backs; the seats have no legs forcing the men to sit cross-legged, and the women to sit with both legs to one-side.

Two bodyguards dressed in black suits, white shirts and black ties with red Cherry Blossom stickpins guard the sliding door. The old man is seated at the far end of the table facing the entrance. Ransom sits with his back to the bodyguards while Sato sits on one side and Kato on the other. No one is wearing shoes.

The door slides open and an attractive young female enters carrying a tray with four glasses and a bottle of *Nabeshima* Sake. She's dressed in an exotic *Yukata* kimono with an *obi* sash tied in a bow in the back. The young woman places the tray on the table. She pours a glass of the Sake and serves it to the elderly gentleman. He nods. The young woman then serves Ransom, then Sato, and finally Kate. After serving the Sake she leaves.

Ransom looks at the old man and then at Kate. She shakes her head ever so slightly.

Ransom: "Carla had me plant a tracking device under the limo. She wants to know exactly where Malcolm goes."

Sato: "We know. We're the ones that gave her the device, but it's not a tracker, it's a bomb."
Ransom: A bomb!
Kate: "Take it easy. It's a fake. It can't detonate."
Ransom: "She was going to blow Malcolm up?"
Sato: "Both of you…"
Ransom: "Why me? She doesn't know who I am, does she?"
Kate: "No, she has no idea who you are. As far as she's concerned you're just collateral damage."
Ransom: "Son-of-a-bitch!"
Sato: "Everything has been arranged. Just keep a low profile and do what Carla asks. Kate will keep an eye on you to make sure Carla doesn't get antsy."

The old man nods to SATO.

Sato: "It's time for you to meet Mr. Shinigami."

Ransom looks at the old man and then at Sato.

Sato: "Mr. Shinigami is Mrs. Shinigami's brother-in-law, and the *Oyabun* of our humble organization."

Ransom looks at Mr. Shinigami. He stands and bows respectfully to the old man, who nods in response.

PART IV

Sakura

Cherry Blossoms

YOU ORDERED THE SPECIAL?
PART I

The Admiral Suite at The Pink Palace Hotel

At two thousand dollars a night for the suite, and another twenty-five hundred for the hooker, this was going to be an expensive evening, but Malcolm didn't care. He was still fuming over his confrontation with Carla. The nerve of that ungrateful bitch after all he'd done for her.

He raised her, treated her like a daughter, and taught her the business. Now she's just going to toss him aside like some disposable appliance that outlasted its usefulness.

What do you expect? Her father was a ruthless killer and her mother was a heartless whore with an iceberg for a heart. He'd spent years under the thumb of Boris Antipov, and there was no way he was going to do the same for his ice princess daughter. The phone on the desk rings…

Malcolm: "Yes… come right up, The Admiral Suite."

A few minutes later there's a knock on the door. He opens it to reveal an exotic blonde Japanese beauty dressed in a black skin-tight long-sleeved mini dress with a plunging neckline almost to her waist. She wears a black ribbon scarf around her neck that dangles down between her breasts. A small black satin handbag hangs from her shoulder. The dress is without decoration except for a red Cherry Blossom pin just above her left breast.

Hooker: "You ordered the special?"

Malcolm takes in the sight of the exotic beauty.

Malcolm: "I certainly did."

Malcolm watches as she walks past him through the living room and stops at the bedroom door. She looks back over her shoulder.

Hooker: "Are you coming or do you want me to perform all by myself?"

Malcolm already feels his seventy odd year old heart pounding out of his chest. The Hooker gets to the bed, drops her purse on the floor, and turns around.

Hooker: "Unzip me sweetie, so I can peel this thing off."

She turns her back to him waiting. Malcolm slowly unzips her dress and as he does, he is a bit unnerved. Her entire back is covered in large red and gray Cherry Blossom tattoos.

As he ever so slowly peels off the dress he sees that her entire back and buttocks are covered in the pretty red and gray blossoms. The dress drops to the floor beside her purse. She's wearing nothing underneath. He carefully turns her around. The red and gray blossoms wrap around her body covering her abdomen and chest. The only parts of her body that aren't decorated are the parts not covered by the dress. The design is completely symmetrical on both sides of the unadorned valley that runs down between her breasts.

Malcolm: "Incredible!"

She's completely naked holding a red Cherry Blossom stickpin in her right hand.

Malcolm: "And what's that all about?"
Hooker: "Oh this? Well you did order the special…"

She jabs the stickpin into his neck. Malcolm raises his arms to her neck, but by the time his hands wrap around her throat, he's already paralyzed. He collapses in a heap. She stands directly over his body and looks down. His eyes are as wide as saucers as he looks up unable to move.

Hooker: "Sato says hello. Not to worry that little pinprick won't kill you. It's just to make you more manageable."

She walks over to the bed, pulls back the covers and messes up the sheets as if Malcolm and her had some vigorous sex. She picks up her dress and slips it back on like a snake sliding back into the skin it just shed. She tosses her purse onto the chair in the corner.

She goes over to Malcolm and looks down at the wide-eyed old man. She takes a deep breath and kneels down unbuttoning his shirt and removing his pants. She drops the pants and the shirt on the chair, picks up her purse, and takes out a syringe. She bends back down over Malcolm running her long elegant fingers over his body and down under his boxer shorts giving him one last thrill. It was the least she could do.

Hooker: "Like I said the little pinprick was just to make you more manageable, however this…"

And she holds up the syringe so he can see it.

Hooker: "This I'm afraid will kill you."

She squirts a little liquid from the syringe into the air. She then injects Malcolm with the rest of whatever is in the hypodermic. She watches closely as his eyes grow bigger until they turn into a blank lifeless stare.

She finds her silk scarf that was still lying on the floor and reties it around her neck. She goes back to the chair and finds the cell phone in her purse. While it's ringing, she searches in Malcolm's pants for his wallet.

Hooker: "Hi, it's me. I'm finished here. Have one of the boys pick me up out front."

She only finds a few hundred dollars in Malcolm's wallet, disgusted; she takes half of it and puts the wallet back in his pants. She starts to head for the door but stops. She returns to the chair and looks in the side pockets of his pants. She finds a fat wad of cash in a billfold that must be at least three thousand dollars. She stuffs the whole thing into her purse and leaves.

YOU ORDERED THE SPECIAL?
PART II

The News Room Bar and Grill

The News Room is a trendy restaurant and bar located in the theatre district often frequented by business executives and members of the establishment movie community. The place is laid out like an old fashion newsroom. There's even a glassed-in printing press that prints a daily newspaper style menu where every item is treated like a news story.

Waiters and waitresses are all dressed in 1950 style suits with pleated, cuffed pants, wide-lapelled jackets, and the most hideous wide ties you'd ever seen. Each server wears a fedora with a press pass jammed into the hat's headband.

Carla Antipov sits alone as usual. The newspaper menu rests in front of her unread. She is not one who enjoys the incessant chatter of inane conversation while she eats. Her evening meal is a time for quiet contemplation of the day's events. Her vice of choice is power. She does have a weakness for abstract impressionist artwork and food that looks better than it tastes, but power is her kryptonite.

A cute young Japanese waitress arrives at Carla's table. She's the same woman Ransom ran into at the Tanoshii Basho Mall who had a fondness for holding hands with her partner. She's wearing the same reporter's outfit as all the other serving staff. The getup includes a ridiculously wide necktie, tied in a Windsor Knot so that the ends fall at least six inches above her thin waist. The tie is held in place by a red Cherry Blossom stickpin.

The waitress flips open the stenographer's pad she uses to take orders. Carla doesn't bother to even look up or to acknowledge her presence.

Waitress: "My name is Sukura and I'm your server this evening. We have a wonderful salmon dish that you might enjoy and a delightful…"

Carla cuts her off in mid sentence.

Carla: "I'm really not hungry. Just bring me a Scotch On The Rocks for the time being."

Waitress: "The chef has been working on a new special item that I can get him to make for you. I'm not suppose to offer it to just anyone, but you look like you could use something special."

Carla thinks the young woman is impertinent but she can't resist something made exclusively for her.

Carla: "What is it?"
Waitress: "It's called a Queen Ann's Lace Salad: very light, you'll enjoy it I'm sure. If not, I won't charge you."
Carla: "All right, bring me the special. And don't forget the scotch."

The Waitress heads for the kitchen. She passes through the swinging doors into a beehive of frenetic activity. Several chefs stand yelling instructions to *sous-chefs* and line-cooks. Waiters come and go placing new orders on racks above each station. They leave with a handful of plates to deliver to waiting customers. The kitchen is organized chaos. The Waitress spots the Chef with the red Cherry Blossom stickpin stuck into his white chef's jacket. He's the same man she was with at the Tanoshii Basho Mall.

Waitress : "One Queen Anne Special…"

The Chef nods and proceeds to make a carrot salad with mint, feta cheese, and a hot chilli paste called harissa. He reaches into his pocket and takes out a spice jar filled with coniine, the active toxin found in Hemlock leaves, the poison of choice for the ancient Greeks. He sprinkles it generously over the salad and tosses it all together. He adds some more feta cheese and shelled pistachio nuts on top. He shouts…

Chef: "Pick Up, Table 4!"

The Waitress grabs the dish and heads out into the dining room. Carla has already finished her second Scotch. The Waitress places the salad in front of Carla.

Waitress: "Here's your Special Miss Antipov."

Carla doesn't notice the Waitress called her by name. She just assumes everyone should know who she is. After all she's an important person; soon to become an even more important person. She holds up the empty glass…

Carla: "Another!"

The Waitress heads for the bar and Carla starts in on the salad. The Waitress waits at the bar while the bartender makes the drink. She watches Carla devour the salad. She thinks to herself: *'I thought the bitch wasn't hungry.'* She waits another few minutes and notices Carla isn't looking too good. She heads for the table with the Scotch. She places it down in front of Carla. She's white as a ghost and her cheeks puff out like she's going to throw up.

Waitress: "How was the salad?"

Carla reaches into her purse hanging on the arm of the chair. She rifles through her wallet looking for cash. Her face has turned green. She staggers to her feet almost knocking over the chair. She throws five twenty-dollar bills on the table.

Waitress: "Are you all right Miss Antipov?"

Carla looks at the Waitress realizing she knows her name.

Carla: "How do you know my…"

The Waitress scoops up the hundred dollars.

Waitress: "Have a pleasant evening Miss Antipov."

The Waitress heads for the kitchen and through the sliding doors. She spots the Cherry Blossom Chef who has changed into his street clothes. He's holding a woman's coat. She does not stop. She walks briskly through the kitchen chaos to where the Cherry Blossom Chef is standing. When she reaches him he helps her on with her coat, He takes her hand and they leave through the back door.

EXTRA! EXTRA! READ ALL ABOUT IT!

An elderly news seller stands in front of his street kiosk filled with newspapers and magazines from around the world. Business executives and office workers scurry past all anxious to get to work. Occasionally one stops to pick up a paper.

Ransom Konnors strolls by and stops.

Ransom: "How are you Harry? It's a beautiful day."
Harry: "The usual Mr. Ransom?"
Ransom: "The usual Harry."

The old man hands Ransom the Times and the Gazette.

Harry: "I hear congratulations are in order Mr. Ransom. Good to know there's still hope for us working stiffs."

Ransom smiles and nods a silent thank you to the old geezer. He tucks the newspapers under his arm and looks up at the television in the corner of the kiosk.

The TV weatherman cracks some inane joke that the newsreaders overreact too. Ransom turns to go to his new office at The Bolshoy Land Development Company.

As he walks away, he hears the news…

News Reader: "Papers were filed in court yesterday revealing chauffeur Ransom Konnors as the only surviving relative of the late Bol'shoy Boris Antipov. With the untimely death of Carla Antipov, Konnors inherits the Bolshoy Land Development Company, a major player in the redevelopment of downtown

LA, and the new owner of the Tanoshii Basho Mall.

Konnors assumes the role left vacant by the recent passing of long-time Chairman Malcolm Sokolov, while his half-sister Kato Kimura takes on the duties of company President; also announced were the appointments of Mr. Enma Shinigami and Mrs. Sato Muonna to the Board of Directors.

In other news… Mayor Charles Langley formally announced his candidacy for Governor…"

THE END

追伸

TSUISHIN
POSTSCRIPT

Some of the names and references used in the book are taken from legendary Japanese mythological creatures and spirits. The names help to describe the personalities of several characters and to define their roles in the story.

Yakuza (Ya-8, ku-9 za-3): literally means 893, the losing hand in the blackjack-like card game called *Oicho-Kabu*, and of course, it refers to Japanese organized crime syndicates.

Sukura: The Cherry Blossom is a symbol of life's fleeting nature and symbolic of sudden death.

Muonna: A vengeful spirit who has lost her child.

Shinigami: the grime reaper, or God of Death

Enma: King of Hell

Obaasan: Japanese grandmother

Oyabun: (father): head of a Yakuza organized crime organization.

Onna-Oyabun: female Yakuza boss

Chi-san: club manager.

Gozu: (Ox-Face) is a creature with a man's body and an ox's face, that along with his partner **Mezu** (Horse-Face) guard the underworld

Futakuchhi-onna: the legendary two-mouthed wife with an insatiable appetite.

Baruku shokuhin: bulk food

Tanoshii Basho: Pleasant Place

Shizukana Basho: Quiet Place

Bratva: (brothers, brotherhood) a Russian term used to refer to organized crime groups (i.e. the Russian Mafia)

Ty che blyad? Suka blyad!: What the fuck? Motherfucker!

Yebat Suka!: Fucking Bitch!

Cine City

JERRY BADER

CINE CITY

THE WIFE

Beverley Hills, California

Terry Richards, an attractive thirty something woman, dressed elegantly, sits in the back of an airport limousine as it pulls into the circular driveway of an exclusive Beverly Hills mansion, home of Bobby and Terry Richards. Terry pays the driver plus a generous tip.

Driver: "Thank you very much Mrs. Richards. Tell your husband I really enjoyed his last movie."
 Terry: "You're sweet, but my husband doesn't need anyone inflating his already oversized ego."

Terry gets out of the car and enters the house.

Home of Bobby and Terry Richards

A very nervous maid rushes to the door to take Terry's suitcase and coat.

Terry: "Is something wrong Maria? You look pale. Are you sick?"
Maria: "No Mrs. Richards…"
Terry: "Well if everything's okay, please fix me some lunch. I just couldn't eat the swill they served on the plane."

Terry starts to go up the elegant winding staircase.

Maria: "Why don't you come in the kitchen, you must be starved?"
Terry: "I just want to clean up and get changed first."

Terry continues up the stairs.

Maria: "I don't think you should go up there Mrs. Richards..."

Terry stops in her tracks and gives Maria a hard look.

Terry: "That son-of-a-bitch is here, isn't he? Who's he with... that Aussie Slut he's been banging?"

Terry marches up the remainder of the stairs, down the hall to the double doors of her bedroom. She stops to catch her breath and compose herself. She straightens her elegant designer dress and opens the door. The Aussie Slut is sitting atop her husband riding him like Red Pollard whipping home Seabiscuit to victory.

Terry: "Jesus fucking Christ... you couldn't just fuck her in an alley somewhere, you had to do in our bed."

The Aussie Slut jumps off Bobby Richards while in mid moan. She starts grabbing her clothes as Richards causally sits up in bed. He reaches for an e-cig on the bedside table, takes a big drag, and blows out a series of well-formed vapour rings.

Bobby: "Jesus, Terry, don't be so dramatic. Couldn't you have waited till we were finished?"

Terry looks at her husband with utter contempt. The bile in her stomach starts to rise into her mouth. She looks at the Aussie

Slut who is struggling to get into her clothes. Terry shakes her head in disgust. Her gaze returns to her husband.

Terry: "You're such a fucking asshole, Bobby, I mean this time you've gone too far. In our own bed for god's sake. I'm filing for divorce, and when I'm finished, you'll be lucky if you can get a job doing summer stock in butt-fuck-nowhere."

Terry turns her head and calls.

Terry: "Maria! Where the fuck's my lunch?"

THE THUG

The Basement of the El Desnudo Strip Club

Tuco Jannaro looms over a bruised and bleeding Joey Watkins slumped in a rickety wooden chair stained in blood. The man's hands are tied together behind his back. TUCO is dressed in a black Silk Shantung suit cut in the trim Savile Row style over an open neck custom-made Egyptian cotton shirt. On either side of Tuco are large tough-looking men standing silently waiting for instructions.

Tuco: "See this suit... Silk Shantung. Made by one of those highfalutin English Savile Row snobs, but hey... they make one fucking fine suit. So here's a fun fact for you to impress your friends with the next time you're at one of those fancy Hollywood parties."

One of the thugs interrupts Tuco's story.

Ruddy: "I don't think this *cabron* will be relating any fun facts to anybody, anytime soon."
Tuco: "Ruddy, please, don't interrupt. Our friend here needs some sartorial advice. This information could come in handy if he ever wants to upgrade from those cheap knock-off rags he wears."
Ruddy: "Yeah he'll need something nice when they lay him out in one of those cheap pine boxes."

The other thug smirks his approval of the comment.

Tuco: "So where was I? Oh yes, Silk Shantung... this here fabric, my friend, comes from Shandong China, now you got to understand most of the crap people buy comes from China, but that stuff is shit. I'm talking real *basura*. But this here Silk Shantung… it's the real deal; them old time Chinese potentates used to wear this shit before the Commie assholes put everybody in sack-cloth.

Now you wear this type of fabric you can't be hanging out in basements beating the crap out of assholes that don't pay their debts. You just can't do it… cause this kind of fabric wrinkles like crazy. I mean if you spend thousands of dollars having some stuck-up British queer shove his hand up your crotch so you get that Daniel Craig silhouette, you don't want to look like you just got up from a three day knap using your fucking Silk Shantung suit for PJs.

And that my friend, that's exactly what you've done to me. You've made me look like I just got out of bed wearing my very expansive, imported, custom-made Silk Shantung suit. Now you can understand why the fuck I'm so angry. I suppose I'll just have to send the suit out to be dry-cleaned. Now maybe that thief who runs the sweat shop on Main ruins my suit; or maybe he loses it; or maybe he sells it to some schmuck looking for the Mercedes Benz of suits at a Yugo price.

So let's recap: not only do you owe me one shit pile of dough, you've caused me the indignity of wrinkling my beautiful black, British-made, Silk Shantung suite, made from the finest fabric straight off the boat from Shandong Province. And that upsets me no end. And you, my friend, don't want to do that, do you?"

Joey groans an unintelligible answer.

Tuco: "What did you say? I didn't fucking hear you."

JOEY THE PRODUCER

The Offices of JW Film Production

Joey gets off the elevator looking like he just went ten rounds with Mohammed Ali. He walks gingerly down the corridor to his seedy office. He opens the half frosted-glass door with JW Film Productions hand-lettered in black Bank Gothic on the glass. Sitting behind an old wooden office desk is the beautiful and perpetually cheery Jeanie Phillips, his loyal and loving, girl-everything.

Jeanie: "Oh my god, Joey! Did Tuco do that?"
Joey: "It's no big deal honey, no big deal…"
Jeanie: "I'll get you some ice."
Joey: "Yeah ice… but add a lot of Scotch."
Jeanie: "Jesus Joey, it's 10 AM.
Joey: "So?"
Jeanie: "You don't want to be smashed when Bobby Richards arrives."
Joey: "Bobby Richards? What are you talking about?"
Jeanie: "He called 9:00 AM sharp, demanded a meeting this morning. I told him you might be late, but he insisted. He'll be here any minute."
Joey: "Don't screw around Jeanie. I'm not in the mood."
Jeanie: "No joke, Joey. Go get cleaned up. You look like shit."
Joey: "You're serious? Bobby Richards is coming here?"

Jeanie nods her head and smiles.

Joey: "I wonder what he wants?"
Jeanie: "Could be your big break."

A diffused figure appears on the other side of the glass door. There's a tentative knock. The door opens and Bobby Richards, hotshot film star, pokes his head around the door.

Bobby: "Is this Joey Watkins' office?"
Joey: "Mr. Richards, please come in…"

Bobby gives Jeanie an appreciative look, lingering his gaze on her generous cleavage. He returns his gaze to Joey.

Bobby: "What the hell happened to you?"
Joey: "It's nothing just a minor fender-bender on the way in this morning."
Bobby: "Look, I really need your help with a project. Is there somewhere we can talk?"
Joey: "Lets go in my office where we can relax. Jeanie, get Mr. Richards an espresso, or whatever he wants."

Bobby's gaze returns to Jeanie, as his mind toys with what she could provide that he would want. Joey interrupts his gaze…

Joey: "This way Mr. Richards…"

THE DEAL

The Private Office of Joey Watkins

Joey ushers Bobby into his cluttered, shabby office. The walls are covered in posters of cheap screamer flicks. His desk is piled high with dog-eared scripts and headshots of attractive actresses. Joey scurries around the office tiding up piles of debris from late nights working on his latest B-grade project. He picks up several recent issues of *Variety*, a few old *Racing Forms*, and a pizza box with pieces of gnarled crust protruding. He tosses everything into a waste-paper basket.

Joey settles into a worn leather chair that resides behind his desk while Bobby tries to find a clean spot to sit. He chooses one of the two wooden straight-back chairs across from Joey. Jeanie places a steaming espresso on the desk in front of Bobby giving him an enticing view of her well-rounded assets.

Joey: "Well it's certainly a pleasure to meet you Bobby, I can call you Bobby can't I? After all, I feel like I know you so well after seeing all your films. That last one, *The Warrior Peasant* was a humdinger. I didn't know you could blow that much shit up in ninety minutes…"

Joey prattles on until Bobby interrupts him.

Bobby: "Actually that's why I'm here. These big blockbuster action movies are all the same and there's little, or no, acting involved. The studio won't even let me do my own stunts in case I get hurt. Where's the artistic merit in that?"
Joey: "Yeah but it's cool and you're making a lot of dough."
Bobby: "Sure, sure it's profitable but I need a change. The next

new hotshot is just around the corner, and then I'll be yesterday's news… now's the time for something new, something different. Like Bob Dylan in reverse: electric to acoustic, if you catch my drift."

Joey: "Of course that makes sense, but Bobby, are you sure… you're at the top of your game. Besides, let's face it, at your stage, you could go to the big boys and they'd welcome you with open arms."

Bobby: "Maybe… maybe, but even if they did, they'd want me to produce one of those big budget projects; and they'd demand I act in it… that's not what I want, and that's why I came to you."

Joey is dumbstruck, but he's smart enough to keep his mouth shut and listen. Jeanie is carefully taking notes in the corner sitting on a cracked brown leather sofa littered with files and scripts.

Bobby: "I want to start small, low budget but quality you understand… It's all about the experience. See if producing is really for me."

Joey: "Sure Bobby I get it. Test the waters sort of thing. Make sure it's what you really want. Things don't go right, you go straight back to the blockbusters… no harm, no foul."

Bobby: "I'm willing to have my lawyer send you a check today if you're willing to make a movie with meaning, something with soul… something with integrity."

Joey: "And you'll star in it?"

Bobby: "Hell no. I don't even want a producing credit. In fact I insist not having anything to do with the movie, and definitely no credits. I just want to make art, give something back in return for all my success. You can understand that can't you?

Joey: "Bobby, are you sure about this?

Bobby turns his head towards Jeanie, his eyes focusing on the sweet spot between the exposed portions of the two rounded mounds protruding from her dress.

Bobby: "Sure as Miss Jeanie has the prettiest blue eyes in Hollywood."

Jeanie blushes.

Joey: "What kind of split we looking at?"
Bobby: "Fifty-fifty, I think that's fair, after all, you're doing all the work. I'm just putting up the cash. But you got to move fast. I want this thing in production. Have you got a script?"
Joey: "Sure, sure, I got lots of scripts. In fact I know the perfect one."

Joey hasn't a clue what script to promote. Most of the stuff he gets is crap. He desperately looks over at Jeanie who's frantically shuffling through a pile of scripts. She finds what she's looking for at the bottom of the pile, pulls it out, and holds it up for Joey to see.

Joey remembers the script, *The Dead Eye Dick*. It's horrible. It makes no sense, and the plot's got so many holes in it, the screenwriter should have called it *The Swiss Cheese Dick*.

Joey: "That's it, that's the one, *The Dead Eye Dick*! It's a real hidden treasure, a gem of a script… it's a mystery but with soul, real sensitive shit. You want to read it?"
Bobby: "Nah, I trust your judgment, that's why I'm here. You're the professional. I'm just the money. *The Dead Eye Dick*… yeah, that'll work."

Joey: "Jeanie, what's the writer's name, Kandinsky... like the artist, something like that..."
Jeanie: "It's Belinsky like the old ball player."
Joey: "That's it... Belinsky, Jake Belinsky... Get him in here and sign him up. We'll start work right away. Maybe get him to do a polish, you know, pump up the arty side a little. We'll Paddy Chayefsky the shit out of this baby...

Hay what you think... we'll shoot in black and white, high contrast, goofy angles and stuff... old school Film Noir... Kinda Orson Welles meets Francois Truffaut. We'll make it so fucking arty people will want to put a frame around it and hang it on the wall."

Bobby: "Sure, sure, whatever you think, just get it in the works fast. My lawyer will send over the contracts this afternoon."

THE SCREENWRITER

Venice Beach.

Joey and Jeanie in his restored Karmann Ghia pull up in front of Kasha's Kitchen and Bikini Boutique, an orange painted two-story Venice Beach local hangout. The joint somehow combines a diner experience with the sale of brightly colored swimwear presented by skimpily clad waitresses serving such delicacies as all day breakfasts and muffins the size of small pepperoni pizzas. Joey is on his cell phone with Tuco.

Joey: "Tuco, I got your money. I'll drop it off tonight at the club. Listen, what are the odds on the Gonzales fight? Really... Gonzales is that much of a dog. What time's the fight... 9:30? Okay, double me up on Gonzales. Don't worry about it. I'm not interested in another visit to your basement. I said I got the money. I'll be there, 9:00 PM. Save me a table. I think that money I owe you will be coming right back to me by the time that fight is over. Yeah, yeah... don't you worry, I just came into some heavy dough."

Joey hangs up.

Jeanie: "Joey what are you doing? You need that money for the movie."
Joey: "Don't fret baby, the Champ is finished. He's been hit in the head so many times he needs a compass to find the center of the ring. Besides, Gonzales is under-rated. He's bigger, faster, younger, and smarter than the Champ."
Jeanie: "But Joey it's not your money. If you blow it, what the hell are you going to tell Richards?"

Joey: "It's okay. Don't worry, I'm not betting all of it, just enough to get us some nice new digs, and maybe a little vacation in Europe or someplace. Hey, I win that bet maybe we go to Cannes and mingle with the fat cats. This is our big break, honey. Things are turning our way. Come on let's sign up that hack writer and get the ball rolling."
Jeanie: "I don't know Joey, you blow this deal and I've got rethink our relationship…"
Joey: "Jeanie honey, I got it covered. Stop worrying, you'll give yourself an ulcer. Now… you sure this is the address. It's a diner I think, or maybe a boutique? I don't know what the hell it is. Are you sure this the right place?"
Jeanie: "This is the address on the script, and it's the same address Jake gave me over the phone."

They park the car and enter Kasha's Kitchen and Bikini Boutique. Very attractive waitresses wearing colorful skimpy bikinis scurry around the busy restaurant delivering fancy omelets and four-digit calorie-count muffins.

An aging female hippy dressed in jeans and a *Strawberry Alarm Clock* tank top approaches them from behind a counter while *Incense and Peppermints* plays over the sound system.

The hippie proprietor may have a few wrinkles,, but she's got the body of a twenty-year-old, and the face of a retired super model. Her best days may be behind her, but she's still miles head of most of her generation, a demographic that has long since gone to seed.

Kasha: "Hi I'm Kasha, I'm afraid there'll be a bit of a wait. Today's Half-Price Muffin Day so the place is packed."

Joey: "Actually we're looking for Jake Belinsky. He said this is his office."

Kasha reaches for a small fuzzy-headed mallet hung over a medium sized Chinese Gong that stands on the counter. She strikes the gong causing the patrons to all cheer, some even stand to applaud.

Joey and Jeanie just look on in amazement. Out from the back comes a forty something man in dark Roy Orbison glasses, a black long sleeve shirt, and black trousers all covered in what looks like flour, at least that's what Jeanie hopes it is. In unison the packed restaurant crowd including the bikini-clad waitresses all start to chant.

Crowd: "Muffin Man! Muffin Man! We all love the Muffin Man!"

Jake raises his arms to his side and bows gracefully acknowledging the epicurean adoration of the crowd. He motions with his hands for the crowd to sit. They obey.

Kasha: "They all like their muffins…"

Jake slowly makes his way to the front where Kasha, Joey, and Jeanie are standing. Kasha kisses Jake on the cheek in what is obviously a, *he's mine*, display for Jeanie's sake.

Kasha: "Jake baby, these people asked for you."
Jake: "You Watkins and Phillips?"

Joey and Jeanie nod. Kasha returns to her duties manning the cash register.

Joey: "Is there somewhere we can talk?"

Jake sprinkles white powder like pixie dust all over Joey's leather jacket and Jeanie's abundant cleavage as he gestures to a corner table marked staff.

They make their way to the table and cram in tight with Jeanie sandwiched between Joey and Jake. Kasha arrives with two mugs of hot coffee and two humongous sized muffins. Jake puts his hand on Jeanie's thigh under the table…

Jake: "Try the muffin gorgeous, they're one of my specialties. Each one packs a bit of a surprise."

Jeanie ignores the muffin but digs the spike of her high-heel into Jakes's black calfskin cowboy boots. He doesn't flinch, but he does remove his hand.

Joey: "So down to business."

The meeting continues with some talk about Jake tightening up the script and moving a few things around to try to plug some holes in the plot. The meeting ends with Joey giving Jake a check and Jake promising to deliver the revised script in a week.

THE LAWYERS

The Boardroom of Nick Scurilla, Divorce Lawyer

Terry and Bobby Richards face each other across a large boardroom table at the upscale Wilshire Boulevard offices of Divorce Lawyer, Nick Scurilla. Terry's lawyer, Scurilla, is the leading divorce lawyer for disgruntled Hollywood wives.

Scurilla wipes invisible lint off his ultra expensive midnight blue custom-made chalk-stripped suit. He looks dapper in his imported red silk tie and black Italian Gucci loafers. He lounges casually beside Terry Richards fussing with his gold Rolex watch. Across the table is Bobby Richards, smug and confident. Beside him is his showbiz lawyer Manny Sharpe who watches his opponent with amusement.

If Nick Scurilla is the primping venomous Lionfish of divorce lawyers flashing his showy tentacles in an arrogant display power, then Manny Sharpe is the ugly, lumpy Stonefish, indistinguishable from a rock, but even more deadly than his ostentatious adversary. Sharpe's suit may be as expensive as Scurilla's but on Sharpe it looks like a wrinkled thrift shop special.

Scurilla: "That brings us to the community property: the house, investments, and cash assets."

Sharpe pulls a piece of paper out of a manila folder that resides in a well-worn brown leather attaché case. He pushes the paper across the table toward Scurilla, who looks down at the piece of paper and slides it over for Terry to see.

Scurilla: "What are you guys trying to pull? According to this the house is mortgaged to the hilt; the cash in the bank hardly covers monthly expenses; and the only other asset is this investment in some movie property: *The Dead Eye Dick*?"
Sharpe: "That's it. That's all there is. Bobby and Terry have been living the good life for a long time, and money only goes so far when you live like that."
Terry: "That's bullshit, Bobby! You got more money than Midas. Where the hell have you stashed it?"

Scurilla puts his well-manicured hand on top of Terry's, to calm her down a bit.

Bobby: "That's it baby. That's all there is. Exotic cars, first class weekend trips to Paris to pick up a few things, designer dresses, it all adds up."

Terry start's taking the bait but again Scurilla intercedes before she can speak.

Scurilla: "So what's the deal with this movie investment? Since when do you produce your own movies?"
Sharpe: "Bobby's not getting any younger. It's time he looks to the future. He can't be doing all these action movies forever. *The Dead Eye Dick* is a way to diversify."
Scurilla: "This isn't going to fly, Manny. You guys are going to have to do better."
Sharpe: "Look Nick you can't get blood from a stone…"
Scurilla: "That's what you think…"
Terry: "You're a son-of-bitch Bobby… after all these years this is how you want to end things. You're the one who slept around. I've been a good wife."
Bobby: "You're right honey, I'm the bastard, I admit it…"

Sharpe: "Bobby will you keep quiet and let me handle this…"

Scurilla: "Let the man talk."

Bobby: "It's okay Manny. I want to do this. Terry is right. She's been a good wife. I'm the villain here."

Sharpe: "You're doing this against my advice!"

Scurilla: "Bobby you got something to say, now's the time to say it, or else we'll see you in court."

Bobby: "I'm willing to give up my share of *The Dead Eye Dick* project. Terry can have the whole thing. Forget community property. I just want to be fair."

Terry: "You're really willing to turn it all over? No strings?"

Bobby: "No strings Baby, You can have the whole enchilada. I'll tell you this: it's a winner, a real gem: a fucking hidden treasure. It'll make a shit pile of dough. You'll be set for life."

THE BET

The El Desnudo Strip Club

Joey enters the Desnudo Strip Club at the appointed time. He's more than a bit nervous carrying a Hello Kitty backpack filled with fifty thousand dollars in a room full of wise guys and strippers.

The room gives off an eerie glow from the reflection of pink, mauve, and blue neon lights that bounce off every shiny surface. Most of the dancers and waitresses are nude except for g-strings that cover very little and do-me heels that threaten to give the girls nosebleeds.

A friendly pole dancer hanging upside down notices Joey's backpack as he passes…

Pole Dancer: "Love the knapsack, Joey… You brought your own dinner? What's the matter? Don't you trust Tuco's food?"

Joey smiles a nervous smile as he continues to makes his way through the crowded club to a room in the back reserved for VIPs. The room is filled with Tuco's cronies, his best customers, and the prettiest girls the club has to offer.

The women are making sure all the men are spending money drinking and having a good time as they watch the last of the preliminary fights on a sixty inch flat screen television. Tuco, his bodyguards, and two dancers are at a cubicle in the back.

Tuco: "Hay… look who's here, right on time for a change. And look what he's brought… now isn't that the cutest thing you've ever seen."

The bodyguards and dancers all laugh.

Joey: "I think you going to like it."

Joey drops the backpack on the round black table littered with various half-empty glasses of booze and various bottles of expensive vodka and champagne. Tuco looks at the backpack and smiles. He leans forward and slides open the zipper a few inches to peek in side. He closes the zipper and tosses the bag to one of his bodyguards.

Tuco: "Have Lenny count it, just to make sure nothing accidently on purpose slipped out a hole in Miss Kitty's bottom."

Tuco gestures to Joey to sit down beside one of the dancers who cuddles up close beside him placing a glass of champagne in his hand.

The room quiets-down as the main event is about to start. The boxers are introduced and the bell rings to start round one. Gonzales comes out swinging. He's all over the aging Champ.

Gonzales backs the Champ into the ropes with a flurry of lefts and rights followed by a vicious upper cut that all but puts the Champ out, but the ropes manage to hold him up. Everyone in the room and at the fight are on their feet yelling and screaming at the Champ to fight back.

The referee gives the Champ a standing eight count. Blood trickles down the side of his face. The Champ nods he's okay to continue. The ref orders the fighters back to the center of the ring.

Gonzales comes on hard again with another flurry of punches staggering the Champ again. Gonzales knows the Champ is finished; a cut has opened over his other eye, and blood flows freely down his cheek.

Gonzales backs off, savoring his moment in the spotlight. He dances around the ring in celebration, but the Champ is still standing. Waiting.

Gonzales gears up to finish off his opponent. He comes at the Champ just like before with a battery of lefts and rights to be followed by a final uppercut kill shot, but this time the Champ is ready for him. As Gonzales winds up for the final blow, he sees the Champ's left hand coming straight at his head. That's the last thing Gonzales remembers until he wakes up in the dressing room ten minutes later.

Tuco is bent over laughing his ass off. Joey is dumbfounded. Tuco still laughing turns to Joey.

Tuco: "Well I hope Kitty's got another package ready for me…"

Joey doesn't say a word. He just gets up and leaves with the sound of Tuco and his crew still laughing.

Tuco: "Tomorrow Joey… I want that package tomorrow, or it's back to the basement we go."

TUCO'S OFFER

The Office of JW Film Production

A month has passed and Joey has continued to lose money to Tuco. Joey is running short of the funds needed to produce the movie.

Joey, nervous and fidgety, sits behind his desk staring at Tuco who's seated in one of the straight-back chairs across from him. Ruddy stands behind him, arms crossed. Jeanie stands off to the side clutching a stuffed Betty Boop backpack. Tuco looks at Jeanie and what she's holding.

Tuco: "What's a matter? You ran out of Hello Kitties? Never was much of a cat person myself… more of a dog man I guess. Actually, I prefer Betty Boop anyway if you really want to know. She's sexy… isn't that right Ruddy."
Ruddy: "Yah boss, she's sexy. She has that *je ne c'est quo* thing going on."

Joey looks at Jeanie.

Tuco: "See honey, we really are a classy operation. Even the help knows French shit like that."
Joey: "Jeanie, give Tuco the bag."

Jeanie hands Ruddy the bag. Ruddy peeks inside to make sure it's stuffed with money, and not just old newspapers.

Tuco: "Joey… you know I like you, otherwise Ruddy wouldn't have been so gentle with your late payment penalties. Besides, for the last month or so, you've been paying up pretty regular. But really Joey... you should get a new hobby cause gambling is just not your thing. Maybe you should be concentrating on that new Bobby Richards' movie you've been working on."

Joey: "How d'you hear about that?"

Tuco: "Oh... I hear things. Word gets around about stuff like that. Maybe I'd be interested in a piece of the action. Say you turn over your interest in the Bobby Richards' flick and I forgive the rest of the money you owe me."

Joey: "Trust me Tuco, you don't want any part of this dog. It's a loser Tuco. Believe me."

Tuco: "Who you trying to kid, Joey? Bobby Richards' movies always make money, big money."

Joey: "Yah but this isn't really a Bobby Richards' movie. You see it's..."

Tuco: "Cut the crap Joey, the more you object the more I know this movie's a winner."

Joey: "Tuco please, you got to..."

Tuco: "You think about it Joey. I figure a few more bets and you really won't have much of a choice, anyway. It's either the movie, the money, or..."

Tuco turns and looks a Jeanie, practically salivating all over his Silk Shantung suit.

Tuco: "... it's the beautiful Miss Jeanie Phillips, your choice Joey."

Tuco gets up, and straights his suit. "Fucking Silk Shantung shit, wrinkles like an old whore on crack. Next time I go for a nice lightweight Italian wool, maybe Zegna. This Chinese shit always looks like you slept in it. You be good Joey and think about what I said. And take good care of Miss Jeanie cause I got a feeling we'll be seeing a lot of one another.

Tuco and Ruddy leave Joey's office.

Sitting in the reception area is an attractive middle-aged hippie chick with the body of a Victoria Secret model and a forty something man in dark glasses, a black long sleeve shirt, and black trousers speckled with the remnants of white power. Tuco notices the couple waiting, paying special attention to the white substance on the Johnny Cash wannabe. Tuco elbows Ruddy as they leave…

Tuco: "I think I know how Joey is financing is hobby…"

Jeanie comes out of Joey's office. She sees Belinsky and Kasha and waves them into the inner office.

Joey, Jeanie, Bekinsky, and Kasha are discussing production issues.

Joey: "Listen Jake I know how much you want this movie to get made but we're running out of money. We got a cast of nobodies and a director that just got out of rehab, and we still don't have enough dough. We can't even afford food service."

Belinsky looks at Kasha sitting beside him; she touches his hand gently and nods.

Belinsky: "Don't you worry about food service Daddy-O… dough is my specialty. Kasha and I will provide everything you need: all day breakfasts and muffins for everyone."
Jeanie: "Well they say breakfast is the most important meal of the day."

Joey: "Yah, and I like muffins."
Kasha: "If you like muffins, you're going to fucking love Jake's."

A OFFER HE CAN'T REFUSE

The El Desnudo VIP Room

Joey sits in a black leather chair in the El Desnudo VIP Room. Ruddy stands at the entrance of the room blocking anyone from entering or leaving. Tuco lounges on a black leather curved sectional with two of his most attractive dancers, one on either side. He causally cleans his fingernails with a razor sharp Bulldog tactical knife. The pink, mauve, and blue neon lights envelop the room like a surreal translucent shroud.

Tuco: "You brought the rest of the money?"
Joey: "I'm a little strapped for cash right now. You know how it is with this Bobby Richards' movie and all."
Tuco: "Sure Joey I know how it is: once a deadbeat, always a deadbeat. And you were doing so well… paying up like a bitch in need of a fix."
Joey: "You got to understand Tuco, everybody on set needs to get paid or they'll walk, and then we're both shit-out-of-luck."
Tuco: "Yah Joey, I get it. Everybody wants to get paid including me. The difference is, none of your dopey actors have a Ruddy."
Joey: "You'll get your money. Don't I always pay up?"
Tuco: "Why don't you hit-up Richards for some more dough?"
Joey: "I already tried, no chance."
Tuco: "Well that does narrow your options a bit."

Ruddy moves away from the door and comes up behind Joey; close enough that Joey can smell the garlic from the meatball grinder Ruddy had for lunch. Joey turns his head slightly to see where Ruddy is standing.

Joey: "Don't worry Tuco. I'll get your money."
Tuco: "Oh, don't misunderstand my friend, I'm not worried…
not worried one bit."

Ruddy puts a giant bear-sized paw on Joey's shoulder. Ruddy's fingers dig deep into Joey's clavicle causing him to wince in pain.

Tuco: "I'm not worried because you got options: you can pay me my money, you can deliver Miss Jeanie Phillps on a platter, or you can sign over your interest in that Bobby Richard's movie."

Ruddy's fingers loosen their grip for an instant, but before Joey can catch his breath, Ruddy's arm wraps around his neck lifting him six inches off the chair. Joey can't breathe.

Tuco untangles himself from the two women draped all over him. He gets up from the sectional still holding the Bulldog tactical knife in his right hand.

Ruddy still has Joey in a modified sleeper hold. Tuco takes the sharp end of the Bulldog and touches it to Joey's forehead just hard enough to leave a red mark.

Tuco: "You know I like you Joey, you know, because if you were anybody else, we wouldn't be talking about options. Now I like my Betty Boops, and even my Hello Kitties, but today you show up with no bags at all. So Joey my friend, if you were anybody else, the only bags we'd be talking about would be body bags."

As Tuco talks he runs the Bulldog down Joey's forehead, between his eyes, and down his nose leaving a thin red track.

When Tuco reaches the end of Joey's nose with the Bulldog, he places the sharp end of the knife in Joey's right nostril.

Tuco: "You ever see *Chinatown*, Joey? Great fucking movie. There's this scene where Roman Polanski threatens Jack Nicholson; I love that scene. You know the scene I'm talking about, don't you Joey?"

Joey nods as best he can under the grip of Ruddy's arm.

Tuco: "So Joey… what's it going to be: Betty Boop, Jeanie Phillips, or Bobby Richards?"

Joey tries to speak but can't. Tuco signals Ruddy to let Joey go.

Joey: "I'll send over the Bobby Richards' contracts this afternoon."
Tuco: "I knew we could come to an equitable arrangement, after all, that's what friends do. Right Joey?"

MAGIC MUFFINS
I LOVE THE SMELL OF MUFFINS IN THE MORNING

On The Set of *The Dead Eye Dick*

The scene takes place in a church. High wattage Redhead and Blonde movie lights, microphones on long boom arms, and an assortment of other equipment and technicians litter the sanctuary. Joey, Jeanie, and Belinksky watch from a balcony high above the sanctuary floor. Everyone on set is stoned.

The actor playing the Hero is dressed in a drench coat, Borsalino fedora, and a black eye patch. He stands inside the church doors looking down the long aisle to where another actor dressed as a Priest waits holding a cardboard box.

The Director is passed out in a director's chair at the back of the church. Remnants of a Belinsky muffin encircle the chair like a satanic warning to keep away.

A snoring alcoholic Bum sleeps in a pew only a few feet from where the Priest is standing. No one has bothered to remove him from the shot.

Joey: "What the hell? Isn't anybody going to get rid of that Bum?"
Jeanie: "Everybody looks stoned."
Joey: "What did you put in those muffins?"
Belinsky: "It's my special formula, straight out of the Alice B. Toklas cookbook."
Joey: "Jesus Christ! They're high!"

The Assistant Director, a kid that looks twelve but is actually twenty-five and a recent dropout from film school, has taken charge. He stands behind the Cameraman barking orders while waving one of Belinsky's muffins around in the air, periodically taking a bite.

Assistant Director: "Action!"

The Hero walks slowly down the isle towards the Priest in what is supposed to be the climatic scene of the movie. The Cameraman, wrapped in a Steadicam rig, follows the Hero as he walks. The Assistant Director follows closely behind nibbling on his muffin dribbling crumbs all over the shoulder of the Cameraman.

The Hero looks the Priest in the eye for a long dramatic moment. He glances meaningfully down at the box the Priest is holding, and then up into the Priest's eyes.

Hero: "Is that the murder weapon?"

At that moment the Bum stumbles to his feet and stretches broadly, making a loud yawning sound. Everyone turns to look. The Bum stumbles over to where the Priest is standing with the box. He opens the box and sees two of Belinsky's magic muffins.

Bum: "I love the smell of muffins in the morning!"

He takes one of the muffins out of the box and takes a giant bite scattering crumbs all over the Priest's black costume. Everyone on the set just stares; the Cameraman is mesmerized still filming the bizarre scene.

Bum: "Smells like victory…"

The Bum reaches into his dirty overcoat with his free hand
while he takes a final huge bite of muffin. He pulls out a bottle
of cheap wine, unscrews the cap and takes a long swig.
He wipes his mouth with the sleeve of his filthy coat. He
belches loud enough for the Vatican to take notice.

Bum: "Belch!"

He looks back into the box eyeing the last lonely muffin. He
picks it up and sticks it into one of the pockets of his filthy
overcoat.

Assistant Director: "Cut! That's a wrap."

Joey turns to Jeanie

Joey: "Tuco is going to kill me."

THE PRIVATE SCREENING

Joey, Jeanie, Terry Richards, and Tuco sit in a darkened screening room at Terry Richards' home. The end of *The Dead Eye Dick* is playing on the screen in front of them…

Bum: "I love the smell of muffins in the morning!"

The Bum takes one of the muffins out of the box and takes a giant bite scattering crumbs all over the Priest's black jacket.

Bum: "Smells like victory…"

The Bum reaches into his dirty overcoat with his free hand while he takes a final huge bite of muffin. He pulls out a bottle of cheap wine, unscrews the cap and takes a long swig. He wipes his mouth with the sleeve of his filthy coat.

Bum: "Belch!"

He looks back into the box eyeing the last lonely muffin. He picks it up and sticks it into one of the pockets of his filthy overcoat.

THE END

The credits start to roll.

Tuco: "What the fuck was that!"
Terry: "What is this… a joke?"

Tuco grabs Joey by the collar and lifts him out of the expensive black leather theatre chair. He starts shaking and swinging Joey around like a Pit Bull with his favorite sock puppet.

Terry stands with her hands on her hips fuming at her ex husband's mean spirited scheme to trick her out of a fair divorce settlement.

Terry: "I'll kill the son-of-bitch!"

Tuco bangs Joey into the wall a few times causing a number of large framed Bobby Richards' movie posters to go off kilter.

Tuco: "Get in line lady. I'm going to kill the little prick first."
Terry: "Not that prick you idiot, my husband… He's the one that set this whole fucking scam in motion."
Tuco: "Your husband… Bobby Richards?"
Terry: "My ex husband…"

Tuco has Joey a foot off the ground pinned up against a wall with one hand while holding off the hysterical Jeanie Phillips with the other.

Terry: "Will you let go of him for Christ's sake, before you break something!"

Tuco releases his grip on Joey. Joey drops to the floor in a heap. Jeanie kneels down beside him making sure he's all right.

Tuco: "Your husband set this whole thing up just to screw you out of a divorce settlement?"
Terry: "That's exactly what's he's done."
Tuco: "Jesus, lady, I thought I got screwed."

Tuco turns to Joey and Jeanie who are both still on the floor.

Tuco: "Don't think this lets you off the hook you little prick. You still owe me the money."

Jeanie looks up at Tuco from the floor beside Joey.

Jeanie: "We'll get you your money, but we want our interest in the movie back."

Tuco laughs.

Tuco: "You want it back? It's yours, for all it's worth. I wouldn't wipe my ass with this piece of shit. You just get me my money."

Tuco storms out of the house.

Jeanie looks at Terry.

Terry: "You got an idea?"

Jeanie nods.

Terry: "How about a drink?"

JUST DESSERTS

The Martini Shot Eatery

Paparazzi crowd the busy sidewalk in front of The Martini Shot Eatery, Hollywood's latest hotspot. It's a place where deals are done and reputations are made. Exotic automobiles, more expensive than most people's homes, stop in front of the restaurant.

Tuxedoed valets and car jockeys rush to open doors to what seems like a never-ending procession of Gucci, Fendi, and Versace.

Each new arrival is greeted with an explosion of electronic flashes and screaming fans. The beautiful people dash to The Martini's welcoming entrance flashing their dazzling white capped ivories, while the ladies show enough hot flesh to melt the lens on a photographer's Hasselblad.

As each guest enters the ornate carved double wooden doors designed to keep the riffraff at bay, they are handed the restaurants signature concoction, the Lychee Martini: a vodka lychee juice, and vermouth mixture designed to settle the nerves, wet the appetite, and loosen the tongue.

Jeanie, Joey, Belinsky, Kasha, and Terry Richards sit at a dark maroon suede banquette that surrounds a centre stage table reserved for the most favored quests of the evening. The table is littered with great reviews of *The Dead Eye Dick*, and predictions for the upcoming award season. The champagne is flowing freely. Studio heads, a-list actors, and directors stop by in an endless stream of congratulatory sycophancy.

With Jeanie's assistance and the potent power of Jake Belinsky's mind expanding treats and snortable party favors, Terry Richards was able to convince her movie insider friends to get *The Dead Eye Dick* played at a variety of prestigious film festivals. Their hope was to get a distribution deal that would generate enough money for Joey to payoff Tuco, and for Terry to pay her divorce lawyers.

To everyone's surprise the critics loved it. One influential newspaper raved:

"The Dead Eye Dick is a brilliant merging of Altman's stream of conscious adlibbing and Fellini's baroque fantasy montages delivered by a fabulous cast of newcomers that rival Cheech Marin and Tommy Chong's laid-back comic brilliance."

Another important Hollywood scribe wrote:
"Joey Watkins? Jake Belinsky? WTF! Who knew brilliance could be found at a hippie muffin shop."

In the end Terry Richards ended up with more money from the movie than she would ever have seen from a reasonable divorce settlement.

With his share of the profits, Joey was able to payoff Tuco, and parlay *The Dead Eye Dick's* success into a three-picture deal with a major studio.

Jake Belinsjy quit screenwriting to devote full time to expanding Kasha's Kitchen and Bikini Boutique into a nationwide muffin empire despite being under investigation by the FBI.

And finally Jeanie Phillips got what she wanted, a new last name, and Joey's community property.

THE END

Killer Jazz

JERRY BADER

RUM PUNCH!

Flugelhorn Jazz Club, Los Angeles, California

The sound of jazz filters through from the club into the bathroom cubicle. A well-dressed man stands propped up against the wall of the bathroom stall. His eyes are closed as if enjoying the pleasures provided by the woman kneeling in front of him. The scene is unremarkable if not for the blood seeping from the hole in the man's forehead and the matching stream of red that leaks from the gap in the back of the woman's expensive hairdo.

Leon Bailey sits by himself in the back corner of the Flugelhorn Jazz Club. He's a tall, elegantly dressed, coffee-colored gentleman with a deep baritone voice and a refined Jamaican accent. He's dressed in a bespoke black chalk striped suit and an open-necked white Egyptian cotton shirt.

On stage are four musicians: a drummer, floor bass, saxophone, and pianist. At the piano is Maurice Digits Delbourne, the son of legendary reggae icon Dickerson Delbourne, murdered on stage during the Harmony & Peace Concert: a rally intended to calm the violence that surrounded the feud between the two major Jamaican political parties.

Bailey and Delbourne are old friends and anytime Del is in town, Bailey makes sure they get together for a few drinks and some killer jazz. Tonight the music is as sweet as ever, but Bailey is distracted.

He writes something on a napkin with his Black Delta Serena fountain pen and places the note under his Rum and Coke. He signals to an attractive blond waitress in a tight, low-cut mini dress with a slit up the side, just in case her other attributes distracted you from noticing her long, stylishly hosed legs. He adds a fifty on top of the note.

Bailey: "Don't turn around. Keep looking at me…"

He taps gently on the fifty with his finger several times. The waitress's eyes move to the fifty and back to Bailey.

Bailey: "There are two black men sitting near the stage; one on either side…"

The waitress almost turns her head to look, but she catches herself.

Bailey: "Good girl… There's another one at the table right behind you. See if you can find out who they are."

The waitress nods ever so slightly; swivels smoothly on her six-inch stilettos, and heads for the kitchen.

Ask Bailey what he did for a living and he'd tell you he was *maitre de* at the Montmartre Gallery Bistro, which was true as far as it went. To be more precise, Leon Bailey was the senior operative for Bobby Bloom, an ex French DGSE agent who happens to run the Montmartre as a front for his private investigation service, specializing in solving sticky problems for movie industry big shots like ex mobster Arnie Bernado.

The waitress appears almost magically beside Bailey. She gracefully leans over the table as if to collect his empty glass, her head close to his…

Carol: "I think they might be cops… they're all carrying guns, but it's weird… they've got accents like yours, but not so nice, kinda rough like."

The waitress reaches for his empty glass. Bailey puts his well-manicured hand gently over the woman's.

Bailey: "Take the note and slip it to Del as soon as you can."

Bailey places another fifty under the empty glass.

Bailey: "They're not cops… and they're definitely trouble. Deliver the note and get the hell out of here… fast."

Carol: "Thanks…"

The young woman scoops up the empty glass, the note, and the two fifties. She stuffs the bills in her bra and moves quickly to the bar where she orders two 007s, a potent mix of Bacardi O, Orange Juice, and Sprite. The drink was named after Desmond Dekker's ska standard: a concoction that made you feel like Daniel Craig but act more like Jerry Lewis.

Carol moves quickly to the stage with the drinks; she places the napkin on Delbourne's piano directly in his line of sight. Del glances at the note and then at the waitress never missing a beat. He nods. She places one of the drinks on the napkin. As she turns, she sees the man on the left side of the stage push his chair back and reach into his jacket. Carol moves around the stage and positions herself behind the thug.

The music stops and Delbourne turns to the applause erupting from the well-heeled crowd.

Delbourne: "If you dig the sound, the CD's available at the front desk. Gotta keep those ex-wives happy. Stay cool my friends… catch you on the flip side - Peace, Love, and Harmony."

Delbourne athletically hops off the small stage as the two assassins stand and draw their guns. Carol takes the 007 that's in her hand and smashes it hard on the head of the gunsel standing in front of her.

The other gangster moves toward Delbourne but the piano player is too fast, and he hits him in the face with the other drink, splashing a mixture of rum, orange juice, and blood all over the horrified woman sitting in the next table.

The punk sitting behind Bailey, fires a shot into the ceiling panicking the already hysterical audience. With his Barak SP21 in hand, Bailey wheels around catching the third villain in the mouth, knocking him backwards unconscious, along with a few stray teeth that land on the floor beside him.

The first assassin begins to recover from Carol's assault, but she acts quickly by driving the heel of her six-inch stiletto into the side of his neck, spurting blood all over the shoes of the poor woman who's already covered in rum, orange juice and blood. As the mayhem settles and the audience scrambles for the exits, the only ones left standing are Bailey, Delbourne, and Carol, the sexy waitress with killer looks and heels to match.

KILLER SHOES

The aftermath of the attempted murder of Maurice Digits Delbourne at the Flugelhorn Jazz Club.

Detectives Grist, Dime, and Alvarez show up at the club along with a cadre of uniformed cops and crime scene techs. The place is a shambles, the people are frantic, and the police are running around like Max Sennett characters trying to take statements and preserve evidence.

Bailey, Carol, and Delbourne sit quietly in the corner waiting. Carol's hand absentmindedly finds Bailey's; she squeezes hard seeking assurance, Bailey responds in kind. The three bad guys have been taken into custody and are on their way to the hospital with Carol's victim in critical condition. Grist and Dime approach the threesome.

Dime: "What the hell Leon? Are you trying to start World War III?"

Velma Dime is one good-looking dame, something she has a hard time hiding under leather jackets and tailored slacks. But don't let the looks fool you, she's as tough a cop as her partner, Joe Grist, a handsome man with a reputation in the department, and a sweet-spot for his partner; despite the fact she's the girlfriend of Leon Bailey's boss, Bobby Bloom. Grist focuses on Carol.

Grist: "The punk with the hole in his carotid, what the hell did you hit him with?"
Carol: "My shoe."
Dime: "Sweet!"

Grist: "Speaking of sweet, did you notice how he smelled?"
Carol: "Orange juice."
Dime: "Orange juice? They were drinking orange juice?"
Carol: "No, they were drinking Gin and Tonics, but I hit him with a 007."
Grist: "What's that?"
Carol: "Bacardi O, Orange Juice and Sprite."
Dime: "If it's a 007 shouldn't it be 7Up?"
Carol: "They use Sprite."
Grist: "That doesn't make any sense. It should be 7Up."

Delbourne imitates Geoffrey Holder. "7Up… it's the UnCola!"

Everyone looks at Del. "What? Doesn't anybody remember Geoffrey Holder?"
Bailey: "What are you talking about?"
Grist: "Relax… you three are in the clear, everybody confirms the punks were trying to kill Delbourne, but don't be taking any long trips, cause this thing could have repercussions."
Carol: "Jesus… what does that mean?"

Bailey gives her hand an extra squeeze.

Bailey: "Don't worry. It'll be taken care of. Nothing is going to happen to you."
Dime: "You can trust Leon. He'll look after you."

Coming through the door flashing his credentials and heading straight for Bailey is the familiar face of NSA Agent John Smith.

Bailey: "Who invited him to the party?"
Smith: "I knew if I waited long enough your fancy Jamaican ass

would get in trouble."
Bailey: "Always the gentlemen Smith; murder any war heroes lately? Bailey knows Smith from a previous confrontation involving his boss, Bobby Bloom and a dead USAF Major.
Delbourne: "I don't know who the hell you are, but this man saved my life."
Smith: "Yeah… just what the world needs: another pinko musician, who wants to play politics."
Delbourne: "Sorry… I don't know that tune. Perhaps you could whistle it out your ass, so we all can enjoy it."
Smith: "So tell me Digits… you here to raise money for your commie brothers? Say, are you in this country legally, or did you sneak in on a banana boat?"
Dime: "You're outta line Smith!"
Grist: "Look asshole, this is a police matter. You have no authority here, so fuck-off."
Smith: "Well aren't we testy? Besides, aren't you two homicide dicks? No one died here… not yet at least! Despite the little lady's best efforts. Killer shoes by the way sweetheart, you should get them registered as a deadly weapon."

Alvarez joins the group.

Alvarez: "I guess you haven't seen the bathroom?"

Everyone turns to Alvarez.

Alvarez: "One Stone Moss and friend, dead from single gunshots to the head, while enjoying *flagrante delicto*."
Delbourne: "*Kiss mi neck*, Stone's my manager."

Grist turns to Smith.

Grist: "Major Crimes asshole… it's our case."
Smith: "I guess you're just not in the loop. The three amigos your friends here messed with are members of the Tivoli Rain Posse, a political action group with connections to the conservative party running to preserve democracy and the free market system in Jamaica."
Delbourne: "They're fascist gangsters… an international extortion and drug cartel."
Smith: "Not like dear old Rasta Daddy, who just loved his *ganja* and revolutionary brothers. Word is your commie pals want you to run in the next election… and Uncle Sam doesn't think that's a good idea."

Delbourne rises to confront Smith, but Bailey and Grist stop him.

Smith: "You be careful Digits, that's what they call you, isn't it? Stupid name if you ask me? They are more TRP where tonight's threesome came from. Fact is, they'd be doing Uncle Sam a favor, but then, we don't want any civilians to get caught in the middle. Tonight was just a warm-up, so some advice: stick to playing your little ditties, and leave the politics to the adults.

Have a nice life piano man… for as long as it lasts. You won't always have Blondie and the waiter around to protect you."

A BABYLON SYSTEM

Harmony and Peace Concert, Kingston, Jamaica

Six months earlier Dickerson Delbourne stood on stage at the Harmony & Peace Concert. A local Kingston soccer field was converted into a concert venue in order to accommodate the thirty thousand wildly enthusiastic fans that crammed onto the playing field and adjacent stands.

Dickerson and his people organized the free event to calm the violence that was getting out of hand. As much as the senior Delbourne wanted to keep the concert politically neutral, it became clear that, that was not going to happen.

He had to make a choice: allow the conservative ILP, backed by the Tivoli Rain Posse to sponsor the concert; or choose the left of center PFP, backed by the Springer Lane Posse.

Both gangs were deep into drugs, extortion, and gun running with satellite operations in LA, New York, Toronto, and London. The financial wherewithal from each group's illegal activities provided influence with, and cover from, their political allies. Dickerson felt he had no choice but to go with the PFP who even tried to get him to run for the party leadership, but he declined. Instead, he concentrated on music and his message of peace, love, and harmony

Dickerson was coming to the end of his opening set and was about to begin his most popular hit. As soon as he played the first few notes, the audience responded with wild cheers and thundering applause. He was gratified that his fans still craved the sound of his mellow voice but saddened by the fact his son Maurice was on tour and unable to attend.

He looked out over the passionately loyal audience to signal the soundman stationed about thirty feet from the stage on a platform that rose high above the jam-packed crowd. Instead of seeing his engineer, he spotted a TRP hit man aiming a sniper rifle right at his chest. He knew this was it. His status as an icon would be sealed in blood. He thrust his arms wide, letting his guitar hang loosely from the strap. He turned his face skyward to the heavens and roared in defiance.

Dickerson: "Peace! Love! And Harmony!"

The crowd assuming this was part of the performance went wild with excitement while a bullet ripped through his chest. The legendary Dickerson Delbourne was gone.

A PAWN IS TAKEN
CAROL GOES MISSING

Palm Grecian Apartments, West LA, Palm District

Grist and Dime pull up in front of the modest Palm Grecian Apartments in West LA. It's a four-story stucco building with Grecian columns ushering in visitors from a Palm-lined entrance walkway.

The two detectives enter the building and work their way to the top floor studio apartment of cocktail waitress Carol Mason. Dime and Grist are there to carry out a follow-up interview to see if Carol can add any details to her account of last night's events, and to assure her that the target of her weaponized stiletto was going to pull through, albeit with a nasty hole in his neck. As the two cops walk down the hall, they debate the minimal merits of Tacos versus Dim Sum.

Grist: "I feel like Tacos today…"
Dime: "You feel like Tacos every day. You keeping eating that shit and you'll start looking like a Taco."
Grist: "So what do you want to eat?"
Dime: "How about Dim Sum, there's a place around the…"

Both cops stop dead in front of Apartment 316. The door is open just enough for them to see there's been a struggle. They move away from the open door, one on either side of the entrance. Both draw their weapons, Dime favoring a 9mm Glock, while Grist opts for the Italian-made Beretta 92FS. Dime goes to enter but Grist puts out a hand and goes through first. They carefully check the apartment to make sure nobody is hiding. Once they clear the place Dime turns to Grist.

Dime: "Jesus Christ Joe. That's the last time you're going to do that!"
Grist: "What?"
Dime: "You can't keep going in first. We've been partners long enough for you to trust me."
Grist: "I trust you. I just don't want to see you get hurt."
Dime: "I mean it!"
Grist: "Okay… but you get hurt and Bloom will be after me with a hammer."
Dime: "I'll deal with Bobby, you just act like a partner and not a…"
Grist smiles: "… and not a what?"
Dime: "Never mind that, we've got to find the girl."
Grist: "Bailey's not going to be happy. I got the feeling those two had something going on…"

Grist starts to call the station to have the crime scene boys come and take a look to see if they can find anything useful. Meanwhile Dime calls Leon Bailey and warns him not to do anything rash.

Dime: "Leon listen, let us handle this." (pause) "What kind of note?" (pause)
Grist finishes his call. "What's going on?"
Dime: "Just be cool Leon, we'll find her? You just make sure Delbourne is safe."

Dime hangs up.
Dime: "They sent Delbourne a note saying he's got twenty-four hours to announce he's not seeking the leadership of the PFP or else Carol is dead."

THE TIVOLI NEGUS

A TRP safe house, somewhere in West LA.

Randall Wiggins a TRP soldier sits eating an *Ital* breakfast of ackee, plantain, breadfruit, and mango-pineapple juice. Beside the dish of food are a 9mm High-Point pistol and a Kershaw Leek Assisted Opening Blade.

Across from Wiggins sits Carol Mason, her hands tied behind her back. She's wearing a torn kaki work shirt and jeans. Nigel, The King, Solomon, leader of the LA Chapter of the TRP, stands in the corner talking on his mobile phone. Wiggins pushes his half eaten breakfast towards Carol, who just squints at him with a disgusted look on her face.

Carol: "And how am I supposed to eat with my hands tied behind my back?"
Wiggins: "This girl, she be given me the stink-eye, and all I'm try'in to do is be nice."
Carol: "What is that shit?"

Wiggins points to the breadfruit.

Wiggins; "This be breadfruit Blondie."
Carol: "What's it taste like?"

Wiggins stabs a piece with his knife and shoves it in front of Carol's face.

Wiggins: "It taste like bread."
Carol: "Why the hell would you want a fruit that tastes like bread? You want bread… eat bread. You want fruit… eat fruit."

Wiggins pulls the plate back and shoves the giant piece of fruit into his mouth almost cutting himself with the switchblade.

Wiggins: "You should be eaten something Blondie. Put some meat on your bones. Give a fella something to hold on to while he's wail'in."

Solomon hangs up the phone and turns to Wiggins.

Solomon: "Leave the woman alone Wig. You just watch she doesn't try to runaway or nothing."

Wiggins just shrugs, takes the Kershaw Blade, and uses it to pick a piece of ackee out of his teeth.

Carol: "I hope you cut your face off with that thing."

Wiggins laughs so hard he almost knocks his food on the floor.

Wiggins: "Don't you worry your little blond head; you ain't got enough meat on your bones for me to do any carving on."
Solomon: "Knock it off Wig. The lady is our temporary guest. She'll be leaving us... one way or another by tonight."
Wiggins: "You hear that Blondie, you be leaving us one way... or another."

Wiggins lets out a laugh that gradually turns into a violent coughing fit that escalates until Solomon comes to his rescue by smacking him hard on the back. Wiggins finally recovers and gives his boss a look.

Wiggins: "Did you have to be hitting me so hard?"

Solomon: "Nah… I could have let you choke on your breakfast.

Carol smiles, shaking her head.

Carol: "Serves you right asshole. I was hoping you'd gag on that shit."
Wiggins: "That ain't funny Blondie. Maybe we be get'in playful before the day is over."

THE NEWS CONFERENCE

In front of The Beverly Hills Hotel

Maurice Digits Delbourne is standing on a raised platform in front of a cluster of microphones surrounded by cameramen and reporters. On his left are Detective Grist and Dime, and on his right, Leon Baily and his boss, Bobby Bloom. The frenzied media are shooting video and shouting questions creating the usual LA media circus.

Multiple Reporters: "Were you the target at the Flugelhorn? Who was trying to kill you? Was it the ILP? Was King Solomon behind the hit? Are you running for PFP leadership?"

Delbourne steps closer to the microphones and raises his hand quieting the mob of reporters. He puts his hand in his jacket pocket and pulls out a folded piece of paper. He unfolds his notes and reads.

Delbourne: "I am not a politician. I'm a musician first and foremost. I am also a proud Jamaican, born and raised. I am saddened by the recent violence that has followed me to my beloved adopted country, the United States of America. And <u>that</u> is not acceptable.

Like my father before me, I believe in peace, love, and harmony... and therefore, I want to make it perfectly clear that I have <u>no</u> interest in being the leader of any political party.

I will not seek, nor will I accept, any nomination to run in any election... in Jamaica, or in the USA. It is my sincere hope that this announcement will put an end to the violence."

The reporters reignite their barrage of questions.

Multiple Reporters: "Are you a Communist? Are you in the USA legally? Are you going to vote? Are you afraid? Who will you vote for?"

A black Hummer with darkened windows slowly drives up the semi-circular entrance to the hotel. The crowd of reporters stubbornly resists the SUVs urging, assuming it's there to whisk-away the piano player and his entourage.

The front passenger-side window rolls down. An arm extends out the window holding a Glock 18 automatic pistol. Two shots are fired into the air.

BANG! BANG!

The reporters all scramble for cover. Microphones and camera equipment go flying everywhere. Women are knocked to the ground by their frantic colleagues. TV types dive for the bushes without regard for their expensive hairdos.

Bailey knocks Del to the ground as Bloom, Grist, and Dime unload their pieces into the Hummer as it speeds away nearly missing several newsmen, but taking out the iconic hotel entrance sign. Something is thrown out the window of the Hummer as it races down Sunset Boulevard.

A few reporters recover enough to start filing stories while others lay dazed and confused by the sudden dramatic events. Bailey has taken Delbourne into the safety of the hotel while Grist calls the station for reinforcements. Dime and Bloom recover the package that was tossed from the SUV window.

It's a note wrapped around a brick and secured by an elastic band. Dime picks up the brick and reads.

Dime: "You can find Blondie in an abandoned warehouse on the corner of Labrador and Montgomery. – Have a nice day!"

THE SUMMIT

Mort's Delicatessen, Beverly Hills

Mort's Delicatessen is a popular lunch spot for movie and entertainment types. The place looks like something that got stuck in the fifties. The old-school vibe is enhanced by a staff of older Jewish waiters dressed in white shirts, and black slacks covered in crisp white aprons.

Daily specials are delivered with a hint of a Yiddish accent, and a casual disregard for the status of the guest. Special requests from new unknowing patrons are greeted with a terse negative response, and a look of cynical bewilderment at the nerve of such a faux pas. There is a definite air of nostalgia for those guests that remember the studio era's Golden Age.

Sitting at a table tucked away in the back representing the interests of the ILP are Tivoli Rain Posse bigwig Nigel King Solomon and his bodyguard Randall Wiggins. Across the table representing the PFP are Springer Lane Posse leader Harley Wilkens and his bodyguard. At the head of the table is NSA Agent John Smith.

Smith: "You boys have to try the Pastrami in this place. It just melts in your mouth."

The four Jamaicans ignore Smith and the monster sandwiches in front of them. Solomon stares directly at Wilkens who returns the glare with an added sneer. Wiggins and the PFP thug follow their bosses' lead. Smith takes a giant bite of his sandwich coating his upper lip with mustard and stray bits of pastrami. He picks up a napkin and removes the debris.

Smith: "Suit yourselves fellas, but you really don't know what you're missing."
Wilkens: "You want to tell me why the hell we're here? If sitting across from these two idiots didn't make me lose my appetite, looking at you inhaling that heart attack on a plate, sure does the trick."

Smith takes a sip of his Diet Coke.

Smith: "Listen gentlemen we all have a mutual problem that goes by the name of Maurice Digits Delbourne."
Solomon: "We already took care of that issue."
Wilkens: "I wouldn't be so sure about that. The people want him. And what the people want, the people get."
Smith: "Okay fellas, listen up, the two organizations you represent are involved in open warfare, and it's got to stop. Get rid of the piano player and you remove the distraction."
Solomon: "Yeah, and who's going to make us?"
Wilkens: "That's the only smart thing I've heard at this table. Nobody tells us what to do."
Smith: "Without Digits stirring the pot from outside the country, you two can take control. Work together. Share the wealth. There's more money in co-operation than there is in fighting."

Smith jams the last big piece of pastrami and rye bread into his mouth as the four Jamaicans look on in disgust. Smith wipes the last bit of delicatessen flotsam and jetsam from his face. He picks up his Diet Coke and drains the last bit of liquid.

Smith: "Who's going to stop you? I am, that's who. And when I say Me, I mean good old Uncle Sam. Is that clear? The USA has an interest in seeing you two clowns get along."

Wilkens: "Sure that's clear enough, but the citizens of Jamaica might not agree. The man is a second-generation legend."
Smith: "Well that maybe my friends, but near as I can figure, people can't vote for a dead man, can they?"
Solomon: "And who exactly is supposed to make that happen?"

Smith gets up from the table, brushes off a few rye bread crumbs and gives each posse leader a hard look.

Smith: "Oh, you'll figure it out. Think of it as an opportunity at détente. The violence has got to stop. Do I make myself clear?"

Solomon and Wilkens both nod.

Smith: "Thanks for lunch boys. You really should try those sandwiches. They're the best in town."

Smith leaves, sticking the posse bosses with the bill.

DO-OVER AT THE FLUGELHORN

Flugelhorn Jazz Club

A banner stretches diagonally across a large poster of Maurice Digits Delbourne at the piano surrounded by his fellow musicians. The poster dominates the entrance to the club. It loudly declares that tonight is the final performance of the jazzman's current tour.

Delbourne and the rest of his quartet are on stage playing to a standing room only audience. Carol is back at work serving tables. Bailey and Bloom are sitting at a table right next to the stage near the fire exit. Randall Wiggins and Nigel King Solomon are purposefully consigned to a table in the back, creating a buffer of innocent bystanders between them and the piano player. Harley Wilkens and his bodyguard are at the next table. Agent John Smith is at the bar nursing an umbrella concoction.

A handsome well-dressed man enters the club and Carol shows him to a table at the opposite side of the stage to where Bloom and Bailey are sitting. The table is near the entrance to the kitchen and across from the fire exit. Despite being close to the stage it's not a good table. Waitresses scurry back and forth from the kitchen obscuring much of what is going on, both on stage and on the floor of the club. It's a perfect table for someone who does not want to be seen or noticed. The man is Mo Fields, a Beverly Hills tailor who moonlights as a hit man.

Bloom and Bailey both spot Fields as he sits down. Bailey gets up and heads across the club making eye contact with Fields as he passes. Fields watches as Bailey exits the club.

Delbourne is finishing his last set of the evening with a spirited rendition of one of his most popular hits. As the music reaches a crescendo, the audience starts to rise and applaud wildly, hoping for an encore that will extend the evening's entertainment. Fields and Bloom both rise with the crowd.

Bloom starts moving toward Fields as the hit man removes his hand from his suit jacket firing one shot from his Glock into the back of Maurice Digits Delbourne, and another two into the ceiling.

The notorious history of the club was an attraction for many patrons, but the sound of real gunshots was a totally different matter. Confusion reigned; the exact effect Fields was hoping for - hysteria. Patrons run in all directions without regard to exactly where they're going. People crash into tables and knock over chairs causing others to stumble and fall. The foursome of Jamaican Posse toughs look on in bemused amazement, their job is done, and they didn't have to lift a finger to do it.

Bloom makes his way toward Fields just as some wannabe hero tries to grab the hit man's shoulder, but Bloom purposefully elbows him in the head knocking him out cold. The gunman gives Bloom a quick glance as he wheels around on his way to the kitchen. The kitchen staff, busy preparing what they thought would be the evening's after-party desserts, are completely oblivious to the carnage; and to Fields as he makes his way out the back door to the alley, and the waiting black Audi A7. Fields grabs the front passenger-door and gets in as the German sedan peels away down the garbage-lined laneway, swerving violently as it enters the flow of traffic. Fields turns to look at the driver. Bailey returns the look.

Bailey: "Is it done?"

Fields and Bailey both focus their attention on the road ahead as the Audi blends into the usual chaos of LA traffic. Fields replies in a flat unemotional tone.

Fields: "It's done."

MEANWHILE BACK AT THE RANCH

Flugelhorn Jazz Club

The club is a shambles for the second time in a week. The owner sits at the bar weeping at the thought of how he's going to pay to fix the damage, again. The cops and crime scene techs are all going about their business as if this was something they hadn't just done several days ago.

Maurice Digits Delbourne is laid-out on stage with a young female paramedic on top of him, trying her hardest to pound the life back into his lifeless body. If you looked real close, you might have thought the woman looked a lot like Detective Velma Dime. The piano player's fellow musicians and a few patrons stand back watching, hoping for a miracle.

The exhausted paramedic, hair dishevelled, stops. She looks at Grist. He nods. The young woman gets off Delbourne, and two male ambulance attendants lift his body onto a gurney. The female paramedic covers the musician with a white sheet as the attendants wheel him out to a waiting ambulance.

Wiggins, Solomon, Wilkens, and his bodyguard are long gone. Everyone left in the club including Agent John Smith stop what they're doing and watch, as the jazz legend is taken to the morgue.

Smith removes the umbrella from his drink as he slurps the last drags of the concoction from the bottom of the glass.

EPILOGUE: SURPRISE! SURPRISE!

Darwin's Digs, Toronto, Canada

Sam Darwin, aka Maurice Digits Delbourne sits behind a microphone in a glassed-in radio control booth at Darwin's Digs, a newly opened Toronto jazz club. There's a knock on the door and Carol Mason enters carrying a 007 on a tray.

Carol: "Have a good show 'D'."

She places the drink down beside Darwin, co-owner of the club and host of a nightly jazz program, *Origin of The Species*. Carol, his partner, now known as Ann Jennings, kisses him on the cheek and goes back to work supervising the staff. Darwin takes a sip of the rum elixir, and presses a button that starts the show's intro music. He slowly slides a fader up increasing the volume as it fills the jam-packed club.

Darwin: "It's Tuesday and I'm your host Sam Darwin, and this is *Origin of The Species*, a nightly look at the evolution of jazz. So sit-back, pour yourself a nice glass of Jamaican rum, and come along for the ride. You're listening to CJAZ Toronto, where it's jazz all day and all night. We'll be back after a brief word from our sponsor. So stay cool my friend and we'll see you on the flip side."

The Queen Ann Hotel, Yorkville District, Toronto, Canada

Randall Wiggins and Nigel King Solomon sit relaxing in their luxury hotel suite waiting for a call from their local TRP posse contact. Wiggins is continually flipping through the television stations looking for something to watch.

Solomon: "For Christ's sake Wig, you're driving me crazy. If you can't find anything to watch, put on the radio and listen to some music."

Wiggins turns on the radio and starts looking for something he likes when a familiar voice stops him cold.

Darwin: "That was the late great Lenny Breau. Up next is another jazz legend, Django Reinhart. But first we got to pay some bills... so stay cool my friend. Stick another umbrella in the cooler, and we'll see you on the B-side."

Wiggins and Solomon just look at one another.

THE END

ABOUT THE AUTHOR

Jerry Bader is Senior Partner at MRPwebmedia.com, a media production company that specializes in Web video, audio, music, and sound design. Mr. Bader has written and produced dozens of video commercials for clients. Writing scripts and novels is a natural extension that grew out of the experience of attention-grabbing mini movies that focus on the core emotional motivator.

Over the years Mr. Bader has written over a hundred articles on marketing, and he's self-published marketing e-books, hybrid graphic novels, biographies, and a series of children's books. The Neo Noir Hybrid Graphic Novels are story concepts developed with the goal of having them turned into television series or feature films. There are currently ten screenplays, five of which have been self-published as hybrid graphic novels: *The Method, The Comeuppance, The Coffin Corner, Grist For The Mill* and *The Black Crane.*

He's also written *The Fixer* published by Rebel Seed Entertainment. It has consistently been in the top ten percent in several Amazon categories. *The Fixer* is based on the true-life story of a colorful horse racing character. The follow-up to *The Fixer* is the new book *Beating The System* that continues the story of the horse racing legend. Mr. Bader has also written *Organized Crime Queens, The Secret World of Female Gangsters, What's Your Poison? How Cocktails Got Their Names, The Outlaw Rider,* and the soon to be released: *Dead End, Palermo, Stone Cold, The Aussie Switch, and Ballet Of Bullets.*

Mr. Bader has also written a series of children's books, ZaZa Books For Kids, that currently includes, *Two Dragons Named*

Shoe, The Town That Didn't Speak, The Criminal McBride, The Bad Puppeteer, Mr. Bumbershoot, The Umbrella Man, The Ninth Inning, and *14 Ridiculous Tales of Sage Silliness.* All books are available at **amazon.com/author/jerrybader**

www.ingramcontent.com/pod-product-compliance
Lightning Source LLC
Chambersburg PA
CBHW071929190726
48293CB00004B/1211